Bottom of the List

Steve Attridge

D0755460

30130500184048

ESSEX COUNTY
COUNCIL LIBRARY

Published internationally by BeWrite Books, UK.
32 Bryn Road South, Wigan, Lancashire, WN4 8QR.

© Steve Attridge 2009

The right of Steve Attridge to be identified as the author has been asserted in accordance with sections 77 and 78 of the Copyright, Designs and Patents Act 1988. All rights reserved.

A CIP catalogue record for this book is available from the British Library

ISBN: 978-1-906609-28-3

Also available in eBook format.

Produced by BeWrite Books
www.bewrite.net

This book is sold subject to the condition that it shall not, by way of trade or otherwise, be lent, resold, hired out or otherwise circulated without the publisher's consent in any form other than this current form and without a similar condition being imposed upon a subsequent purchaser.

This book is a work of fiction. Any similarity between the characters and situations within its pages and places or persons, living or dead, is unintentional and co-incidental.

Registered trade names are respected, recognised, faithfully reproduced and identified in the text by initial capital letters.

Cover Sculpture by Marc Buisson, © 2009

Hedda — with thanks.

And for my son Jacob and my parents.

Steve Attridge has written stage and radio plays, over a dozen TV series, individual TV dramas, and feature films, including the award winning *GUY X*, starring Jason Biggs and Jeremy Northam. He has also written eleven children's novels and a history book about the Boer War – *Nationalism, Imperialism and Identity in Late Victorian Culture*, published by Macmillan. He has also published poetry and won an Eric Gregory award. He won a Royal Television Society award for best drama (*The Queen's Nose*) and has had two BAFTA nominations (*The Boot Street Band* and *The Queen's Nose*).

In another life he lectured in literature, film and history at various universities and has taught writing courses in the UK, Europe and the Far East. He has also worked as a gardener, a cook in a monastery, and possibly as a dancer, but this is disputed.

He lives in Warwick and Spain, but not simultaneously.

Bottom of the List

Chapter One

Gravity was the real enemy.

It all began when Adam Bittermouth, in his sixteenth year, lost his virginity to Rosemary Puddock in a potting shed in Ealing. His left foot had been trapped dangerously in the blades of a lawnmower and the deckchair, on which he was sitting as she bounced on top of him, collapsed. He thought he might lose a foot as well as his innocence.

He was fraught, anxiety wriggled in his veins, the smell of bodies, grass cuttings, danger and creosote creating a lethal brew that made him feel sick, and searing into some deep cellular level so that forever after grass made him tense and the woody petroleum of creosote gave him feverish sexual dreams that lasted for nights and days.

Then it happened for the first awful time. As her breasts smothered his face, he started to gag and struggle for air. He could feel the roof of the shed bearing down on him; the sheer immensity of gravity beyond the rotund dimensions of Rosemary as it pressed down and threatened to squash him like a bug.

He shouted "Oh Christ, save me!" and ran from the shed, leaving bewildered Rosemary to retrieve her knickers from a bucket of slug pellets. Outside, naked from the waist down and his gelled hair sticking out madly like satellite spikes picking up terrible messages from the ether, he fell to the ground. The sky itself was closing in. Kamikaze leaves crashed to earth, birds struggled against the weight of the universe above them, trees grew rigid and bony in their vertical toil. Everything was bearing down, pushing. It was too hideous for thought.

Gravity was the real enemy. And similar attacks happened often afterwards, unexpectedly, when he would fall to the floor, whimpering. Therapists, counsellors, psychologists and psychiatrists, all manner of experts came and went. They recommended re-birthing, meditation, homeopathic prescriptions, surgery, Zen running, deep massage, hydro baths, psychiatric drugs, the removal of surplus cranial fluids. But all these experts and the terrifying density of remedies seemed themselves to be a force of gravity, weighing him down, pushing against his very tissue, so that he would run away gasping for breath.

One night he awoke and realised what it all meant – he feared death, the darkness crowding and engulfing him and returning his body in one form or another to the earth. That was what gravity was, it was death coming, and in an epiphanous moment he saw it – all the microscopic waves and subatomic energies of gravity coagulated into a single figure, the Dark Invader, death made flesh. This monstrosity was an avenging cocktail of the archangel Gabriel, Darth Vader and Mister Potts, his old primary school teacher who would rap him painfully across the knuckles with a cane, lean in close and with a shocking blast of halitosis, call him a bubonic cretin.

Armed with this new and fearful knowledge, Adam thought carefully. His whole life would now be a quest to keep the Dark Invader at bay. What he needed was a scheme, a plan, and in the course of realising his plan he would leave something of himself behind, something grand and unforgettable. People would look at it and think: Bittermouth. He would still die (though with advances in science, maybe even that could change) but something big that he had achieved and built would remain and, in that, would be a kind of glittering defiance, a solid remonstrance against the mortal fact of gravity. A slap in the Dark Invader's face.

It would have something to do with high buildings, structures, power over others and power in an absolute sense. Also, it must have some noble purpose attached to it: the Law, Medicine, Education.

He plumped for the latter, with its corollaries of wisdom, enlightenment, humanity and expansion. He got a First Class Honours at Cambridge, a quick ascendancy through administrative ranks and now, at only forty-eight, he was Chancellor of Roebuck

University. In the nineteen eighties he had anticipated how the new Thatcherite entrepreneurial spirit would enter education. Be as independent as you can, turn students into consumers, create high return investment programmes, run universities like any good business. It was all now falling beautifully into place. (Though the idea of falling made him queasy.)

His first achievement at Roebuck was to build the now infamous Tower of Light, the tallest structure in the English Midlands, slap bang in the centre of the campus. Forty-two floors of steel and golden glass that shone like the many eyes of God and sent shards of light across the rest of the university complex. It was incongruous and beautiful. No one could see inside. Already it was a place of myth, an Olympus.

People wondered if he existed.

On the forty-first floor was Adam's modest apartment, and above this his office took up the entire top floor. Lofty buildings blew a raspberry at gravity. If only one could keep building, a Jacob's ladder of industrial strength, one could perhaps get beyond gravity itself and look down on the bemused Dark Invader. The ceiling was absurdly high but sometimes, in panicky moments, he would get a stepladder and measure the height from floor to ceiling to ensure it had not diminished, that the Dark Invader did not have his cosmic foot bearing down on it.

His early disastrous experience with Rosemary in the potting shed created an aversion to intimacy, a troubling sense that, somehow, contact with others had led the Dark Invader to single him out. Human propinquity invited the gravity of death and might bring on another onslaught, reducing him again to quivering terror.

Consequently, now that he was in a position of power, he avoided human contact. He never went out and no one came in, and despite a growing tendency to have loud discussions with himself, the result had been fewer attacks. The beauty of technology was that messy human contact was, in any case, largely redundant. The whole world could come to his office via conference videophone, CCTV, computerised messaging and digitalised video links. He could see and talk to people without ever being with them. A high tech dumb waiter delivered tasty morsels and bottles of iced Sancerre. CCTV meant he could see almost anywhere in the university at any given moment. He had microscopic cameras clandestinely installed in light fittings and air vents. He could see all and nobody else was aware.

He knew, for example, that Professor Jim Currant in Chemistry liked to wear only his underpants while marking essays; that the Chief Librarian sometimes masturbated into a yoghurt pot during his lunch break in the staff toilet; that a Chinese student kept an illegal pet rat called Chi in her room. All these nuggets of information confirmed his view that, as far as human beings were concerned, the further away from them he was the better.

The beauty of being so high up was that he could look down on the campus below but not see its cheap red-bricked crumbling modernity – buildings constructed not to last – and could overlay his own mental blueprint of soaring towers with high, reinforced roofs that would withstand missiles and hurricanes. Roebuck would be a city of light and strength. The New Enlightenment would arrive. He had chosen his registrar, Jeremy Pickles, wisely. An ambitious runt who could help Adam realise his vision: put financial structures in place; ensure Roebuck led in any digital initiative; streamline departments; frustrate the Dark Invader.

Education was about defying gravity and ensuring that Adam Bittermouth gave the Dark Invader a run for his money. There would be casualties on the way, but any war entailed casualties, and it was important that the General kept his head. They were already making a start in the soft departments. English was probably the softest of the lot. Adam peered down and thought he could just make out the English department to his left. It looked so puny. A single giant step could crush it.

Chapter Two

Brimley Trevalyan, Professor of Quality Assurance in the Department of English, tried to imagine prunes and apricots.

He was chairing the departmental meeting and Damien Dimmuck – the Creative Writing Director, a failed poet who always wore billowing white eighteenth century shirts with frilled cuffs and tucked into black trousers so achingly tight he walked as if a medium sized rodent had just entered a major orifice – had done it again. He said that since his arrival in the English department, the Creative Writing Programme, or Prog as he called it, had really got its shit together.

Damien's constant references to shit and getting it together had greatly soured Brimley's life. It was a sore reminder of his affliction. His shit was so together it needed an act of divine nuclear fission in his colon to get it moving. His shit wasn't only together, it was solidified into a block so hard it rattled when he moved. What on earth had he done to deserve it? More to the point, what had he eaten? He had no memory of sprinkling Polyfilla on his breakfast cereal or of pouring liquid cement into his tea. Perhaps he did these things in his sleep. Perhaps his wife had discovered the arrangement he had with Nora, the departmental secretary, and it was she who was responsible. If true, it was diabolical. A trifling fornication with a woman of little importance was one thing, but constipation was seriously hard shit, a monumental pain in the devil's impasse.

His day began with apricots and high fibre bran, then a half-hearted prayer to a Catholic God who seemed remarkably indifferent to his bowels, and lots of strong freshly brewed coffee. Coffee apparently worked for a singer called Janet Jackson, so Nora had said. It was an instant enema. The singer even had a sponsorship deal with a coffee manufacturer. A sponsored shit, thought Brimley. Christ, I'd do it for nothing. They could have the lot gratis, if only I could shift it. He moved miserably in his seat, clenching and unclenching his buttocks, and felt as if he was carrying a baby submarine in his bowels.

Damien was now referring to ways of motivating students to get their shit together. It was too much. Brimley woke up Frank Finch and told him to carry on chairing the meeting, then said he had an urgent call to make to his publisher, apologised, and left.

Nora had a huge steaming mug of freshly ground waiting for him. Uncanny how in tune she was with his bowels, and she seemed to have a prescience of the exact moment he would enter a room. He gave her a perfunctory kiss on the cheek (no one was around) and took the coffee to the toilet. He sat down, sipping, and waited hopefully, the mug warming his bony knees. He'd give himself half an hour. If it worked, he might even get some work done today.

His biography of Ronald Drain, eminent children's writer, was proving more difficult than he'd anticipated. He thought it would be a doddle writing up the life of a cranky old wordster who wrote about witches and monsters for toddlers, but it was nothing of the kind. For reasons Brimley could not fathom, Drain hated him, never offered him a drink, and once locked him in the shed where he wrote his books. It had been extraordinary and deeply embarrassing. The memory seemed to stir something below, but then everything tightened and drew in ranks again. Perhaps surgery would be necessary, he thought gloomily.

He wondered how old Frank was doing chairing the meeting. Probably making some fatuous argument for the revival of the semi colon in student essays. (Oh why did I have to think of colons, even semi ones?) Frank would be gone soon. Brimley had been given a chair in the English department not because of the rigour of his intellect but because he was, as the Registrar had confided to him, a bloody good hatchet man. He was professor not because he understood the subtle inconsequentialities of post-post-modernity but because he knew how to shaft underlings.

His brief was simple – to fill the department with cloned

apparatchiks who would advance the interests of Roebuck University PLC and not make waves. That meant getting the old guard out, retaining a few loonies like Mercedes Blonk, whose high public profile gave the department a little kudos, and upgrade the Creative Writing programme by increasing the fees, thereby turning the dreams of the young into hard cash.

Three members of staff were dead wood for the chop, and Frank was one of them. Sacking people, or even better, forcing them to resign, beat sex and came a close second to the infinite blessing of a sturdy bowel movement. Again, Brimley felt a tingle of excitement in that region, suggesting movement, but around it a stubborn wall of resistance.

Chapter Three

He was Pan, a dancing sexual devil, his head in the Enlightenment of Angels and his loins firmly in the world. He had trained an errant curl to flop attractively on his forehead and hide an old chicken pox scar.

He was a great talent. He knew it. The publishing bastards would have to acknowledge it some time too. He had a boyish smile, his wife told him, and despite the flattish nose (surgery might be an option once the university bastards paid him more) and too close-set eyes (surgery might not help here), he'd landed on his feet sexually. Or more precisely, landed on young female students, as often as he could.

Being Director of Creative Writing was an aphrodisiac for Damien – still only thirty-six, no sign of balding, only the merest hint of a paunch – and proved that power had them gagging for it, their little hearts fluttering, their clothes strewn like bunting around his office during special tutorials, their desire to become writers and believing him to be the Sacred Holder of Keys to the promised land of publication and performance making them both vulnerable and extremely willing. It was perfect. And there was still time for him to be discovered as a great writer. (The bastards everywhere were being pretty slow there.)

He'd found a place in the world for now. He thought: I am a man of letters, an adventurer of the pen, a man who can only live intensely in the moment, a creature with the most interesting imagination to the extent that I find it impossible to be truly engaged by any thoughts other than my own.

Words from the future, memorial tributes in their hundreds, fluttered into his mind like a cadence of doves; in The Times Literary Supplement, for example: "*From the earthy tales of Chaucer, through the philosophical sweep of Shakespeare, the divinity of Milton, the intellectual angst of Eliot, the anthropological density of Hughes and the troubled cadences of Heaney to the genius of Damien Dimmuck. His work has restored humanity to itself, taking language into territories of the soul we could only have sniffed at without him."* Could you sniff at territories? Perhaps not. Never mind, he would work on his obituary later.

He smiled as he trounced along the corridor, knowing that from behind, his tightly clad buttocks would be an alluring eyeful for the PhD student he'd carefully placed himself in front of. Timing walks along the corridor was crucial. It could lead to all manner of sexual liaisons. He thought her name was Helga. Norwegian. Big tits. Mole on left cheek. Thesis on Insect Imagery in Seventeenth Century European Poetry. He'd have to mug up a bit on that before he asked her out. Memorise a few obscure lines from some Italian cunt.

And he'd made another good showing in the departmental meeting. "English Studies are in crisis, and what I bring to this place is saving them. Creative Writing is the future," he'd told them. Old Frank had muttered about crisis being a sign of life, then some Latin bollocks about reductio ad absurdum, but he'd ignored it. He was a saviour of sorts. His shit was coming together nicely.

He had a seminar to give: "Finding Your Own Voice." As he'd told Brimley, he taught through personal charisma. As he didn't tell Brimley, the purpose of Creative Writing was not to inspire and create a new generation of writers, but to destroy them. Make them doubt their own abilities, put them off writing, cast little arrows of doubt in the margins of their notebooks, erode their dreams, eviscerate the opposition before it had even got started, and on the way create a bit of an audience for his own work. He was doing them a favour really, because the truth was that most of them were no-hopers. There was also the bonus of getting to shaft a whole bevy of willing young girls. Thank God English was a girl's subject.

Today it was a First Year group, which should have provided a titillating palette of new young bodies, daring to sit near him, bathe in his eloquence, but in fact it had been a bit of a disappointment so far. There was a nerdy weasel-faced twit called Tony or Trevor or something, a fat thing that squatted in the corner, presumably female, but he had no idea of the name, a few more nondescripts, and only one hopeful, a brassy little number from Newcastle called Helen who wanted to "write summat me ma'd be proud of, like. A real workin' class story." It was sweet, really, and mostly they'd stopped people like her coming to university, but she had firm tits and a mouth capable of all sorts of depravity.

He'd flirt with her for a few weeks then suddenly turn his fierce intelligence on her, a blazing concentration of energy that would leave her speechless and naked. Afterwards he would tell her that he would love to leave his wife (she's wonderful, but my intensity exhausts her), but how could he? There was little Eric, light of my life, fruit of my loins … surely he could find a more original, penetrating image, a metaphor so powerful it would define fatherhood for generations. He toyed with it: *dribble of my dick, nosegay of my knob, arrow of my quiver* (here he was in his office thumbing through the thesaurus) … *quosmothrust of my quadrod* (he could fake Latin too), *childspore of my warrior propagator.*

A knock on the door. The great overpowering metaphor would have to wait. It would come to him. Everything would come eventually.

Chapter Four

Frank tried the lavatory door but it was locked. He was sure someone inside said "fuck off" as he turned away, and there were miserable straining sounds from within, but it may have been the dodgy plumbing. It was odd how often new things complained the most, even the plumbing.

This was a new university, yet it seemed to be falling apart. Ceilings had cracks, walls had mould, carpets were stained, people had breakdowns. York Minster, Wells, or any one of the old cathedrals where Frank spent weekends wandering since Margaret had died, seemed robust and dependable. Like the old universities they were friends, and whatever labyrinths of pipes existed remained dutifully silent in them, or gurgled benignly. The plumbing here worried him. It didn't just creak occasionally, it pleaded like a wounded animal to be put out of its pain, and it depressed Frank no end. Then, suddenly, just when the poor creature was about to expire with one final sorrowful lament, it would become an exquisite aria, the plaintive voice in Mozart's *Requiem* rising above all the weight and misery of mortality in a frail expression of hope and life that broke the heart. It was all very odd.

Absit omen, he thought. Let there be no ill omen in these rumblings, as he came out of the toilet and down the corridor, behind a young woman and, a little further on, Damien, for whom Frank felt a dart of sympathy. Clearly, to be walking in such an alarming manner could only signify screaming haemorrhoids. He made a mental note to discreetly give young Damien a gift of Preparation H pessaries.

Five minutes later he knew he was wrong. The rumblings in the pipes were prophetic. All dread and foreboding were fulfilled. All manner of vile pestilence and plague were raining upon their heads in the redoubtable figure of Mercedes Blonk, Senior Lecturer, with whom Frank shared the Third Year Shakespeare and Marlowe course. Frank slipped into the back of the lecture hall where Mercedes, she of the exploding hair, post-feminist dominatrix of the juggling breasts beneath scanty cheesecloth, the Celtic jewellery that rattled like medieval weaponry, she of the late night self-congratulatory chat show, was now in full throttle on *Othello*.

Frank gave most of the lectures because it was understood by now that, with her busy media schedule, Mercedes was always at the university at the right time but on the wrong day, the wrong time on the right day, or not there at all. When she did give a lecture it was to throw the theoretical cat among the pigeons. She once reduced *Faustus* to a personal genealogy of orgasms, which left Frank on a drip at the local hospital for two weeks while he struggled to recover his sanity. Students seemed nonplussed, which was just as worrying. He supposed they had bigger fish to fry than Mercedes's genital machinations – things like student loans the size of Third World debts and campus parking fees for their Fiestas.

"Othello is the ultimate Lacanian moment of latent exchange and desire," she announced as she prowled around the lectern like an overdressed panther. "We know that meaning is never identical with itself, but is a process of division and articulation, of signs being themselves only because they are not some other sign. I am me only in that I am not you," she continued, fixing her gaze on a young Asian lad with the face of a startled fawn in the front row. She moved in closer, reflected in his huge and alarmed eyes.

"You and I enter a symbolic order; as we exchange words we become prey to desire, which dissolves our traditional notions of identity into Otherness. You move in and out of me and I move through and over you. In and out, through and over, up and down, in a cycle of restless longing."

Please God, let her stop, incanted Frank to himself at the back of the hall. Please let her stop. Please destroy her and I'll start going to Evensong again. But today God was not the merciful patriarch of the New Testament, but the Old Testament Jehovah of retribution and pain and punishment. Frank swallowed a painkiller.

Mercedes continued, her eyes scanning the hall for fresh pastures. "So when Othello says to Iago "Would I were satisfied!" we have to articulate the implied question: Is Desdemona a good fuck? Or are we entering into a homoerotic discourse between Othello and Iago, two soldiers, hot as monkeys, prime as goats, used to showing each other their weapons, actually enjoying erotic subtext under the guise of a discussion about marital infidelity. Does Othello really want to give Iago a good stabbing?"

Frank shook his head and held back a tear. That is not what he meant, not what he meant at all, he whispered to himself. Let me not be mad.

Chapter Five

Damien was enjoying the pre pre-coital toying with Helen. He would ignore her for a few minutes then turn his steely blues on her and she would blush slightly. He imagined them on the carpet together, she bouncing on top in a sexual trance, her breasts jigging furiously, almost falling unconscious with pleasure, unable to believe such intense delights were attainable with a man. But not just a man, a poet. Then, afterwards, her stroking his inner thigh, he would gently explain how it could never be anything other than a few erotic and sublimely transcendent moments, and she would cry, but nevertheless be grateful that he had initiated her into such mysteries of the flesh.

He would remain in her imagination, god-like (yes, let's not mince or quibble) throughout her life. Years later, her husband would lie beside her and wonder why she sighed in her sleep in a way she never sighed for him. But she would know. And so would Damien. She would spend hours in bookshops running her chewed fingernails along the many spines: the great yet to be written works: *Flesh Rising* by Damien Dimmuck; *Fresh Wounds From the Front Line* by Damien Dimmuck; *Collected Works of Damien Dimmuck* (a fat tome, this). She would take one of the books and hold it, almost afraid to open it and feel the sacred rush of language reminding her of what she once had, all too briefly.

"Are you all right?" Helen asked.

Damien came out of his reverie and realised he had been sitting there swaying slightly in his chair, the beginnings of an elephantine erection straining painfully at his Calvin Kleins. They were all looking at him. He wondered how long he had been away. Sometimes his imagination frightened him. Sometimes he felt he was the only person in a crowded room who was real. Perhaps it was true. Perhaps in some fundamental way there was only him.

There can only be one, Sean Connery had famously said in *Highlander*. And perhaps it was true.

"I was just thinking of a line for a new poem. It's almost like a religious thing," he said, looking at Helen with what he knew from years in front of mirrors was a troubled, winning look, one that made women want to cushion his sensitivities against the pain of the world.

"Right. Finding Your Own Voice," he said. "I knew even when I was a kid that I had this special relationship with language and had this dream once that Ted Hughes and Seamus Heaney were in my bedroom, looking down at me and Ted was wearing a big furry hat with horns and he pointed at me and said 'You're the one' and Seamus nodded. Always trust your dreams. Finding your voice is like an equation. "

He stood and turned – thus giving Helen a glimpse of his exquisitely clenched buttocks – and wrote on the board with a red magic marker:

EXPERIENCE + TECHNIQUE = AUTHENTIC VOICE

The students wrote this down dutifully.

"I'll read you one of my early poems that made me know I'd found my voice," he said with a little smile. He knew they loved it when he read his work to them. He opened a book entitled *Deep Blood Poems*, published by Big Voice Poetry Press, run by a mate in Milton Keynes in his bedroom. The day would come when the Penguin bastards would be sorry they turned this down. He read, pausing to give each word due emphasis:

"Ten Things That Mean Something

One

Two

Three

Four

Five

Six

Seven

Eight

Nine

Ten."

He stopped and looked at Helen. One of the nondescripts sniffed. Another muttered, "cool." The fat thing in the corner wobbled a little. The nerdy twat stared at her with one side of his face twisted as if he had been given an electric shock.

"What do you think, Tim?" Damien asked him.

The nerd stopped his facial contortions at the fat thing and stared blankly at Damien.

"Trevor. My name's Trevor Bottom."

"Whatever," Damien smiled.

Trevor went bright red and started to sweat.

"If you're going to write, you need to have an opinion," said Damien.

"I thought writing might be a sort of act of discovery. I mean – if it's just an opinion it might as well be a letter to a newspaper or something," said Trevor.

This twat was starting to get on Damien's nerves, especially as Helen appeared to give a little nod when the spotty git spoke. Come to think of it, she wasn't that pretty. Cheeks a bit splodgy and dumpy.

"So you don't like my poem? Come on, I'm a big boy, let's exchange here. Share our shit."

"I just think it's sort of pointless," said Trevor, and grew redder.

"It's ironic, Bottom. It is fucking post-modern irony. Do you not get that?" said Damien.

A few of the nondescripts sniggered at Trevor.

"But it's a bit obvious, isn't it? I mean, the joke's over before it begins really. And you said technique was important and there isn't really any in what you read out. Sorry, I didn't mean …"

"Yes. You did mean it. Don't back down, Bottom. Attitude is partly what gives you a voice." Damien made a mental note that this little turd was going to fail the course outright. "So, how about you? Have you brought anything along to read?"

Trevor went purple and fumbled in his pocket. He took out a scrap of paper which trembled in his hand. Damien looked at him.

He started to read, the sweat dripping down the sides of his nose.

> "This look like acid rain shreds me.
> You in the half-light, half-bright
> Ache of something I stumble to,
> You a tigress in the making,
> A dream-blur in my midnight waking,
> I follow ..."

"What's it called?" interrupted Damien.

Trevor looked up, bewildered.

"I haven't finished ... It's called *Quidnunc* and ...

"Quidnunc? Quid-nunc?"

"Yes, it's Latin. It means one who is curious to know everything, and the poem is ..."

"The poem needs working on, that's what it needs, Bottom. Ruthless editing is what gives a poet his voice. And I'd think carefully before you use a language for doctors and dead Romans. Don't give up the day job just yet, eh? OK, twenty minutes for coffee."

The students trooped out. Damien looked coolly at their retreating figures, and at Helen's arse, which had grown distinctly bigger in the ten minutes since she'd agreed with Trevor Bottom. Once they'd gone, even the fat thing mysteriously managing to disappear, Damien picked up his coffee mug and hurled it at the wall. Bastards, all bastards. Fucking Latin shit. Didn't they want to learn from him? Didn't they want to know anything? Why couldn't they just shut up and listen and admire him, and the pretty ones let him fuck them, and the bastards out there publish him and ask his opinions on the telly? His obituaries would mourn the tragic and untimely loss of he who had given so much, had lived for poetry and love, and been a great man. People always had their own stupid opinions and now he'd got a coffee stain on his frilled cuff. Christ, he needed some coke.

Frank left Mercedes's lecture, almost in tears, and went to the common room to have a cup of tea and a few painkillers. Now he was on his knees beneath the sink, listening to the pipes murmuring melodically. It was a Bach fugue, one theme repeated in a subtle variation of registers. Now in cadence in the dominant key – C Major, he thought. Now repeated an octave higher. Metallic but exquisite.

Damien came in and started washing his sleeve at the sink, trying to remove the coffee stain. If he couldn't, it would mean another trip to Camden Town to stock up on poet clothes. He had on his shades, which he always wore when he felt the world was hostile, even though he couldn't see too well in them. The water increased the activity in the pipes alarmingly and the Bach fugue now became a slaughterhouse where cats were being skinned alive. Frank bumped his head as he got to his feet. Damien looked pale and he remembered the poor boy's affliction. He took a suppository from his pocket and offered it to Damien.

"Take this, dear boy. Just pop it in and let nature do the rest. I can see you're suffering."

Damien squinted at Frank through his shades. Jesus, how does *he* know I'm stressed, he thought. He took what was being offered. It was a bit big, but if it hit the spot, it would do, and he'd taken enough uppers and downers in his life to know they came in all sorts of shapes and sizes. He popped it into his mouth and swallowed, said "thanks" and left. He was going to write a poem and it was going to be a real stinger, he decided. The sodding students could wait.

Frank watched him leave. *De gustibus non est disputandum.* There is no arguing about tastes, he thought, and perhaps the suppository could actually work that way, though logically it would take longer. The bang on his head had started a headache, so he swallowed another couple of painkillers.

Chapter Six

Brimley sat in the Registrar's office, shifting uncomfortably in his seat. The Registrar, Jeremy Pickles, sat opposite, a man whom Brimley thought looked remarkably like a hamster after it had filled its little pouches, and whose front teeth had clearly been designed for a much larger mouth. The Registrar sat on his hands, a habit he'd developed after being told by his public speaking tutor that he waved his arms around so much when he talked that he looked more like a traffic policeman than a public dignitary.

"Are you all right?" he asked Brimley.

"Yes. Why?"

"You just seem to be fidgeting a lot."

So would you if you'd been carting around a ton of consolidated steel in your bowel for nearly five days, Brimley thought. "I'm fine," he said.

"Good. Now look at the big map."

He extracted one of his hands from his buttocks and used a remote control to zap on a large screen that filled the opposite wall. The Registrar loved doing that. It was like being in a war room. It showed a complicated map of graphs and figures and interconnecting lines. The word 'target' appeared a great deal.

"As you can see," began the Registrar, "this is a paradigm of transferability and offers a comprehensive picture of our organizational structures, how we are embedding innovative practices and assisting their implementation, evaluation and procedural guidelines, a time frame for target orientation, facilitation and achievement, and a comparative assessment grid so that we can rationalise key areas that will need restructuring. You're with me, so far?"

"Of course." Brimley was utterly lost.

The Registrar used the remote to highlight a block graph with the word 'ENGLISH' on it. Brimley saw that the block was considerably smaller than others, especially BUSINESS STUDIES, ENGINEERING and MEDIA STUDIES.

The Registrar tut-tutted. "It's bad, but your appointment has made a difference. Income has gained three and a half per cent this academic year. Creative Writing, as part of a soft matrix, is generating a reasonable income, but what we're looking at long term is e-learning and digital repackaging of your course modules."

"Right," said Brimley. Where the hell was this going? "So you want me to ..."

"Exactly. Prepare for a major restructuring. We're looking at a staff cull within five years of twenty-two people in English."

Brimley knew he'd been employed to get rid of people, but this was really radical.

"Twenty two? But there's only twenty three of us," he said.

"Exactly. There would be just you and a library of software. You can offer courses worldwide. A Creative Writing package for Eskimos in their igloos and rich American kids in their penthouses, a theory course for Italian peasants or Guatemalan gangsters, preferably both. We'll be part of a global village with no staffing problems because there will be so few staff, and no students on campus puking and committing suicide every summer. No mess. And a walloping great income for the elite remaining. As Professor of Quality Assurance and only member of the English department your salary will be trebled."

Jesus. This was a big one. And his salary trebled. He was right behind it.

"This is absolutely confidential. I'm telling you because I trust your integrity and because I may need your assistance in seconding certain motions at key meetings which will take place at the newly formed Committee for Research in Academic Practice."

CRAP? If only, if only, thought Brimley. "I'm your man," he said. "I mean, I can see that this is a fantastic opportunity to develop and enhance the intellectual life of the university."

The Registrar smiled and put his hands beneath his buttocks

again. "The Chancellor will be delighted if you can carry this out smoothly. We think of it as the Final Solution."

"Have you … have you ever actually met the Chancellor?"

"Of course. We confer all the time," said the Registrar, thinking that, no, in fact, he hadn't actually met him, but he'd seen him on the video phone. He'd been interviewed that way for his job. One day he hoped to be invited to the forty-second floor of the Tower of Light for sherry. No one had yet, and he was buggered if anyone was going to beat him to it. The view must be phenomenal. Persuading the Chancellor to let him chair CRAP had been a real coup. He knew which buttons to press and told him that most of the research funds would be channelled into a new science park dedicated to the study of longevity. He could almost hear the Chancellor's excitement crackle on the intercom. He had muttered something about gravity and fooling the bastard, but Jeremy lost the thread. In any case, all that was for the future.

"It's imperative you don't breathe a word of this to Fish," said Jeremy conspiratorially. Professor Roy Fish, scourge of administrators, scuttler of secrets, spoiler of plans. Fish had not the slightest fear of Jeremy and was to be watched and kept as in the dark as possible.

Brimley nodded. Fish despised him and publicly asked him what he, Brimley, intended doing when he grew up and learned to speak English properly. He did this in Bittermouth Hall just after Brimley had given his inaugural lecture and was feeling particularly pleased with himself. His ears reddened at the memory of the shame, the titters that rippled around the hall. He hated Fish.

"In the short term we have a new PhD student wanting to register in your department," Jeremy said.

"So what's the problem?" asked Brimley.

"His name is Spinelli. General Spinelli."

"Spinelli? Isn't that …?"

"Yes," said the Registrar.

"But didn't he …?"

"Yes. We won't mention it."

"No, but wasn't there …?"

"Yes, a great deal. Don't mention it. But if we register him he will donate half a million pounds to fund a new research centre. And a further hundred thousand to open the Spinelli Crèche.

"Ah," said Brimley, the penny, in fact half a million pounds' worth of pennies, dropping. General Spinelli, dictator of a small South American Republic, put and kept in power by an American corporation with a sugar cane deal and assisted by the CIA. General Spinelli, famous for the baseball ground massacre of dissidents and his habit of "vacationing" rivals, who were sent on holiday and clearly had such a good time that they never came home. General Spinelli, whose reputed hobbies included sitting up in bed with a couple of mistresses, drinking vodka and watching DVDs of his enemies being poked in their orifices with high voltage cattle prods. All of this was unsubstantiated, of course, because there were few left who *could* substantiate it.

"This generous gift will be of enormous assistance in facilitating our master plan, if you follow me. It will be under the administrative supervision of CRAP, of which I am Chair."

"Yes, but won't there be trouble?" Brimley asked. "Student protests?"

The Registrar smiled. "We're going to announce an increase in student fees and rents on the same day we register the General. What do you think students will be most upset by?"

Brimley nodded. It was no contest. And half a million! There would be a percentage to be creamed off if he agreed.

"The main problem as I see it is that the General wishes to study Virgil's *Aeneid*," said the Registrar.

Brimley's eyebrows lifted. That was Frank's territory.

"But Frank Finch is getting the chop," said Brimley, who was looking forward to the moment when Frank realised which way the cheese was melting.

"Have you no one else who can supervise the General? I mean, surely one of you can translate Latin," asked the Registrar.

But there was no one. They'd got rid of all the Classicists, the Medievalists, the dead wood. All except Frank. All English needed was a few easy novels with a bit of feminist or post-colonial gloss on them, Shakespeare to suggest tradition and class, and Creative Writing to get the punters in. And clearly, in less than ten years, there'd be just him with his own little digital empire.

"We may have to hang on to old Frank for a bit, then." said the Registrar. "Just until the General gets his PhD. We'll put him on fast track and make sure he's qualified within two years. The fewer who know he's coming the better. Obviously, tell no one about the General's … er … generous gift. And we have to keep this away from Fish for as long as possible."

Professor Roy Fish of Engineering was notorious for being able to write the most vitriolic memos in Europe, which often got picked up by the local, then the national press. Professor Fish was a dangerous enemy to have.

"Frank won't be a problem, will he?" asked the Registrar, puffing out his cheeks slightly.

"What do you mean?" asked Brimley.

"I mean he will do it. Won't he?"

"Of course he will. The man's a worm. He'll do exactly what I say."

Chapter Seven

"What do you mean – no?" Brimley was incredulous. Frank was actually defying him. Openly. Him. The hatchet man. Professor Poleaxe. Brim the Destroyer. Professor Cosh. The cloakroom boy – get them in private then scare them witless.

"I mean No," said Frank. "How could I look my wife in the eye?"

"Your wife's dead."

"I was speaking metaphorically. It's out of the question."

"Frank, you are going to supervise his PhD."

"Never," said Frank.

This was baffling. Worrying. He tried rationality.

"Give me three good reasons why we shouldn't register him."

"He's a mass murderer, a rapist and a torturer."

"You're all the same, you narrow minded liberals. Never give a person a break to turn over a new leaf. This could be his chance of rehabilitation, Frank. A few years in a civilised community. Intellectual exchange. Self improvement. That's what we're offering him."

"And what's he offering the university?" asked Frank, his defiance given a heavy narcotic boost by the five painkillers he'd swallowed so far that morning.

Jesus, thought Brimley, Frank is showing native cunning and savvy. This really is a first.

"I don't know what you're getting at," said Brimley.

Frank felt protected by a strange and light-headed sense of distance. Perhaps he'd taken more than five painkillers. The doctor had said to go easy on them, but he may have unknowingly swallowed several extras during Mercedes's lecture.

"I think you do, Professor Trevalyan. This is an internationally known tyrant coming to a university that, like the government, cares more for self image than it does substance. It must be getting something."

Brimley's approach to staff management was edifyingly simple. There were two ways to get people to do what you wanted. You either *gave* them something they wanted, or you *took away* something they wanted. The latter was by far more entertaining, and Brimley was fast approaching the moment of truth with this strange, newly recalcitrant rebel of a Frank.

"Frank, have you been drinking?"

"Of course not."

"Good. This is perfectly straightforward. We are registering a new PhD student and I'm telling you that you are going to supervise him. Do you understand?"

"You can't force me. The Roebuck University Charter states …"

"The University Charter is a piece of redundant toilet paper …" (why did he have to mention toilet paper?) "and has nothing to do with the real world, the one in which I am telling you what you will do."

"And if I refuse?"

"You are out."

"Out? What do you mean – out?"

"I mean sacked, jettisoned, discarded, given the boot, the old heave-ho, your marching orders, the bum's rush, exiled, banished. Sacked. You haven't published anything of note since *The Romantic Disposition* back in the Dark Ages, and some in the Registry might consider you past your sell-by date. One hears things. The Chancellor is not happy. "

Frank turned ashen.

"But what about my pension?"

"Your pension will be a lot smaller. You will have to learn to live on a diet of Classics and yesterday's bread."

"I'll go to the Union," said Frank, the defiance in him receding like a dribbling, weary, tide.

"Ha!" Brimley exploded, warming to his theme. "Ha! How quaint. The Union. That old warhorse with its head and jacksy in the knacker's yard. The Union has as much power in this university as my Aunt Fanny, who is an entirely fictional character."

Frank looked bewildered. The battle had been short, violent and decisive. Brimley tasted victory and it was sweet.

"I'll have to think about it," said Frank.

"Yes, you do that, then come and see me on Friday and I'll give you General Spinelli's research proposal. It needs ... tidying."

Frank stood and left the room like a freshly lobotomised android. And the effect upon Brimley was miraculous – first the faintest of suggestions, then the merest stirring that became an approaching rumble, then a definite undulation, and thirty seconds later he was racing along the corridor and into the toilet.

Students passing outside heard an explosive "Yes! Yes! Yes!" as Brimley celebrated and reflected that decisive management action was clearly the most miraculous laxative in the world.

Chapter Eight

She sat in her room, staring at the abyss. It was always there, beckoning her from inside the old shortbread biscuit tin with the scratched picture of Ely Cathedral on the front, teasing with its chocolaty succulence, its sweet promise of comfort and instant gratification.

The sugary kiss inside the sacred tin was also the poisoned chalice, because no sooner had she devoured the lot – the Picnic Bar, the giant Kit Kat, the Walnut Whip with its creamy insides and nutty nipple, the white Chocolate Buttons and delicious clinginess of the Mars Bar – than she was in hell. She knew about hell, that it was not demons and licking flames, nor was it Sartre's other people, but was the brutal indifference of the mirror and seeing her chocolate-smudged lips and puffy cheeks. Hell was sometimes getting undressed and taking a full look at the worst, the swathes of flesh with wobbling pinnacles and rings of blubber, she exulting like some mad beast in the sheer volume of her own ugliness. She was a bag of fat and, rather than people laughing at her as they did in school, at university it was as if she had become invisible in her vastness.

In the Creative Writing seminar today, the only person who seemed to be even aware of her existence was the strange, nerdy looking boy, who spent most of the time sneering at her. Why didn't he just come out with it and say "How now, fat cow?" if he wanted to mock her? The incessant sneering was painful. But at least it was attention of sorts. Damien, the poet tutor, had not registered her presence once, not in the six weeks of the course. He had never spoken to her, asked her a question, smiled, nothing. She was the largest person in the room, by far, yet the one least noticed.

It was different before Dad died. His death had created a Then and Now. Then was being tubby but loved. Now was being a freak. Her mum had called her that once, on her sixteenth birthday, when she wore the yellow dress. "Cynth, you look like a freak. Like a bleedin' sumo lemon." Cynth had laughed, then gone upstairs, taken it off and shredded the new dress with scissors.

Fat was not a feminist issue, something to be discussed and rationalised, it was being a house of blubber, mountain woman, a chocolate machine. It was real. Once her mum sent her to a counsellor, a patronising woman with doe eyes and the beginnings of a moustache, who said that she needed to learn to love herself and to nurture the person she really was inside. Cynth went out of the session and into the nearest newsagents, then to the park, where she sat alone on a bench and scoffed a Turkish Delight, three Cadbury Flakes, a packet of Maltesers and two Snicker Bars. That was serious nurturing.

She took out her notebook and wrote a few lines about the experience. They were crap, she knew that, but at least it stopped her going to the abyss. She had a whole file of them now, mostly written after binges when the black cloud settled around her and she approached the abyss. Then she wrote a poem to her dad, suddenly angry that he had abandoned her to this world where the bigger you were the less you counted. She most definitely did not love herself. How could anyone love her?

Chapter Nine

Being in love was horrible. It was time to write another list, Trevor decided. He opened his writer's notebook and started two columns to try to understand the contradictory nature of love:

GOOD	BAD
Palpitations	Palpitations
Light headed	Light headed
Dreamy	Dreamy
Unreal feeling	Unreal feeling
Obsessed	Obsessed
Constant sex thoughts	Constant sex thoughts
Sleeplessness	Sleeplessness
Dementia	Dementia

It was confusing. Palpitations were apparently bad, yet they got your blood circulating; feeling light headed was bad for writing essays, but quite a pleasant experience in itself. Feeling dreamy, unreal and obsessing made everything terrifying, but were essential to becoming a great writer. Thinking about sex all the time meant you didn't get much else done, but it was amazing too, even though it meant you spent too much time whacking off, and last week he'd got a nasty blister on his penis. Sleeplessness meant you were constantly knackered, but also created the illusion of life seeming to be longer. Dementia was all right, too, because most great writers were meant to be lunatics. And love was, as Shakespeare said, "a madness most discreet."

So love was a contrary problem and could go horribly wrong. The first time he had seen Cynth, he'd felt a stirring in his loins that slowly spread to his heart. She was all woman, and there was so much of her. He had already made seven lists of things which individuated her, and which now adorned his wall. God alone knew what the cleaners thought was going on, but he didn't care. Love was making him reckless.

There was the 'Fetching Idiosyncrasies' list, which included the way she toyed with a lock of hair that always fell on her forehead, the way she often lowered her eyes as if to retreat into some private world, and the habit she had of sometimes shifting her luscious weight from one magnificent haunch to the other. What this list had taught him was that whatever the beloved does is a small miracle of increased desire, simply because it is her doing it. He noticed everything about her and each time he replayed the memory it was like a small explosion in his groin. He now felt like a walking minefield.

She always seemed to be alone, and that gave her an intensity that made her infinitely desirable. She must be deep, as well as wide. What did she think about? What did she do on her own? He really wanted to know. He really wanted her, but it had all gone disastrously wrong. Trevor had schemed so carefully, and then Damien Dimmuck had ruined everything.

The plan was that at the next seminar, Trevor would screw his courage and smile at Cynth. Eventually she would smile back. There would be a flashbulb-popping moment of mutual recognition, they would go for coffee and everything would be sublime. He would find he could talk to her without making a complete prat of himself and sweating like a pig. He would listen to her and she would realise that no one before had ever cared so much about what it was like to be her, about her childhood, her dreams, her secret thoughts. She would realise that she had never been known before. That night they would go for a McDonald's, have three pints of Heineken each then go back to his or her room to consummate their mutual rapture.

He would crawl over her lowlands, plunge into the great fecund marshes of her middle earth, scale the juggling mammalian heights of her breasts and disappear into them like a deep sea diver. He would exult in the great wastelands of jiggling flesh that were Cynth, and when he finally got there, had arrived, actually done it, he'd plant a flag firmly in her summit. Metaphorically, of course.

The prospect was awesome, thrilling, inspiring, terrifying, and was an essential life-transforming experience if he was to become a great writer. And now it all seemed further away than ever. Perhaps he should go to her now (he sometimes followed her and knew which hall she was in) and declare himself, but what if she wasn't there, or worse, she was there and just laughed at him? Or if she already had a boyfriend, perhaps someone at home called Gavin who wrote her sumptuous letters full of sex and yearning every day, and she was just waiting for the weekend when she could go home to a scorchingly passionate reunion?

How could he find out if there was a boyfriend at home? He could wait until she went out, then break into her room and search for incriminating letters. If discovered, he could pretend he'd had a blow to the head and become disorientated, and might even win sympathy that would transmute into an all-consuming passion. But no, he'd go bright crimson and sweat all over his body and head and no one would believe him. It had to be subtle, he had to think about it, and that meant just one thing – another list.

Chapter Ten

Frank was in agony. He longed for unconsciousness. The burns on his chest and shoulders were smouldering red weals. His false teeth had been taken out and his gums were bleeding where he had ground them together in agony. Rivers of perspiration from his forehead washed around his eyes and stung so he could barely see. Those before him were mere shapes that moved back and forth.

He had stopped pleading hours ago because it did no good and just seemed to make them hurt him more. He was sorry, he was so sorry and would never say 'no' again, never cross anyone, never complain. He would always comply. He would be humble. Anything to make this torture stop. The terrible thing about it all was a sort of intimacy, a perverse contract between torturer and victim. We are in this together. He started to understand sadism, that it was inherently sexual and the inflicting of pain was the fulfilment of desire and longing. The horrible ritual of it.

It made him think of the Old Testament and the piling on of distressing detail, the exulting in pain: "How much more abominable and filthy is man ... he covereth his face with his fatness, and maketh collops of fat on his flanks ... the congregation of hypocrites shall be desolate ... thou shalt make them as a fiery oven in the time of thine anger ... their fruit shalt thou destroy from the earth..." All those insistent imperative verbs. "God is a bloody awful sadist," Margaret had said once, and laughed. Sweet Margaret. "I am weary with my groaning; I water my couch with my tears."

Someone threw a cup of water in his face and his eyes cleared. The General was standing over him, the medals on his chest glinting like cheap jewellery, the thin mouth and ratty eyes of ... Brimley.

Frank awoke with a start. He was soaked in sweat. His head

drummed a beat against his skull. He breathed deeply. This must stop or he'd have a stroke. He reached across to the bedside table and automatically shook a few painkillers from the bottle and swallowed them. In a few minutes he'd feel better. The drumming would stop and become distant thunder, a storm somewhere else.

The thought came unbidden – *There is no God* – and he remembered the first time the notion had struck him, standing over Margaret's grave and cursing the fact that he'd lost his love and his best friend. They had planned a cottage in Norfolk once he retired, for their last companionable years. There would always be his work – the consolations of poetry and the Classics and being part of a great community of minds worth knowing, who cheated death through literature. There would always be that but it would now be in the shadow of his grief, and he knew instinctively that the grief would never die; it would transmute into a thousand other things, but it would never go. He would have to learn to walk alongside it.

He got out of bed wearily. This was the bed he'd shared with her for thirty-one years, two months, one week and three days. It was a pit of snakes now. It was also Friday. He had to see Brimley. He would supervise the General's PhD. But, of course, Brimley already knew that.

The proposal was worse than he thought. It had absolutely nothing to do with literature, showed not the slightest knowledge of Virgil, and was written in English that wasn't so much broken as demolished. Frank scanned the two pages: "This Achilles is good strong man of honour and I write much about his courage and big heart in many wars … I am like warrior too and much common to his spirit … many mens die in this battles but for good reason and them gods know this things." It was infantile drivel.

Moreover, the General's personal statement revealed an alarming Road to Damascus. He stated that after years of "national difficulties", caused by "unworthy enemies of the State", he now had a vision of "love and wisdom" which he believed would be refined by postgraduate study at "one fine English uniservity"

[sic]. Frank, usually willing at least to look for roses in manure, didn't believe a word of it.

"He can't read Latin, he can't write in plain English and he doesn't seem to know anything about the *Aeneid*, all of which would seem necessary precursors to the pursuit of a PhD," Frank said, the tranquillisers he'd taken having given him a semblance of calm rationality.

"But he's passionate about it, Frank. War, warriors, spicy sex. The General has an appetite for the content of one civilization's greatest narratives. That's his intellectual strength, and that's what you have to build on," said Brimley.

"But how is he going to write about the damned thing if he can't read it?"

"You help him. That's your job," Brimley said. "Give the poor man a chance."

"Yes," said Frank meekly. "*Vae victis*."

Chapter Eleven

It was brilliant. It had post-modern edge. It was economical but suggestive, specific but teasingly universal. Damien was chuffed with himself. "Chuffingly chuffed," he said aloud and laughed with the sheer delight in being himself. He settled his thoughts and read it aloud:

> "My mum
> blank as an orange
> fish face through the playground bars
> watching me tiger dance
> to manhood's malice.
>
> My mum
> big body like a wardrobe
> hearing me call
> through the jungle
> of my desires
> for
> sweet
> death."

It was frighteningly good. He might read it to Helen, who was coming for a personal tutorial in an hour. It gave him the confidence he needed to settle another small matter too. He flounced along the corridor. Frank, the damaged looking old tosser who had given him that weird tasting, greasy upper, was just coming out of Brimley's office. Damien knocked and entered. He made his demands: a salary, rather than the six thousand a year pittance he currently received in hourly flat rate terms, and a permanent position. He could always dump it when his book sales went through the roof and he had his own telly programme.

"It's quite impossible, Damien. Your contract is fixed at an hourly rate for the next academic year," Brimley said with a thin smile. He was in no mood to bullshit, and he could actually say bullshit without his bowels hardening. Damien knew Brimley was a tight-arsed git, but he hadn't expected a flat refusal. Didn't he realise how important Damien's work was, how it had saved the English department from being an academic dinosaur in imminent danger of extinction?

"Professor Trevalyan, I have helped this department avoid ridicule and censure. I have put it on the map. The reason we got our ratings shit together is not because of some abstruse article on Horace in a journal nobody reads, but because of Creative Writing. Students are queuing up to work with me. I'm in tune with their souls. I give this department its dynamism. I'm its star turn."

There was no point in false modesty. I've just written a great poem too, he reminded himself. I am the high priest of language, a magician among the young.

Brimley brought his fingertips together on his desk and smiled thinly again. Something was different in him. He seemed more relaxed than usual, as if he'd recently unburdened himself of some great weight.

"You don't understand," he said, knowing that a tone of quiet understatement could produce greater fallout than explosive anger. He read from the CRAP memo he had just received from the Registrar, "'Creative Writing is not about writing at all, it's about targets. We need a) 68.3% students to pass with flying colours, b) at least a 10% publication of student work, which we can always arrange with in-house publications that we referee and approve ourselves, and c) an intake growth of 8% per annum with no further expenditure.' I quote verbatim from the Registrar. Creative Writing is all about target attainment and keeping within the present budget. My hands are tied."

"But you need me," said Damien. "I'm the bloody Director of Creative Writing at this university. It's my show."

It was time for a cloakroom job. Threaten to take away

something. If this went well Brimley could even hope for another bowel movement, which was becoming slightly, though not yet painfully, overdue.

"Either you deliver, Damien, and stop making a fuss, or you're out. There are plenty more failed writers ready to step into your shoes who'd be grateful for a few thousand quid. Let's be realistic, shall we? Now, if there's nothing else, I'm rather busy."

Damien's mouth opened and he gaped like a dying fish. Had Brimley just called him a failed writer? Had he dared to suggest that Creative Writing could actually survive without him? He, who only four years ago had a milestone work, *Basic Urges,* published by Ostrich Press (run by a mate in Watford). He, who had opened the doors of perception for hundreds of students, who had initiated twenty-one First Year girls into the sacred mysteries of the flesh. He was a great man. A poet of significance, a man set apart from, yet also of, the people. He danced with angels and supported Sheffield Wednesday. And this creature had dismissed him as a failed writer who should be grateful for a few lousy quid at this poxy university. He left, stunned. He needed to regroup. He needed someone to restore his sense of self.

It was as if his head had been hammered with a large stone until all proper consciousness and sense had departed. He staggered into the lift. Some great mass wobbled in the corner. Perhaps he was imagining it and his mind had temporarily gone. No. It was the fat thing from his First Year group. Without thinking he pushed against her, lifted her several chins and kissed her violently. He held his lips clamped firmly over hers. He lifted her sweater and grabbed a large breast with his right hand. Then he heard the lift stop and the doors open and he pulled away. God, if anyone saw him kissing this lardy lump his reputation would be shot.

He had done it because he needed something to make him feel real again and it, she, happened to be there. Now it was holding out something to him. He took the offering mechanically and got out of the lift. The doors closed and he looked down at what he held – a folder with POEMS scrawled on it. Oh Jesus, she had given him her fucking poems to read. He'd made the mistake of kissing her and touching her up and now she'd entrusted her godawful bloody life's work to him. Did she really think he would read it? He just hoped she'd think it was all a dream. It hadn't happened, not really, not in any meaningful way. Yes, the scene in the lift never happened. Bollocks. He felt worse now. It was just one thing after another.

The weird old git, Frank, was walking along the corridor to his room. Perhaps he could talk to him. He needed to talk to someone. He didn't trust himself to be alone, and Frank was half senile anyway. He could treat him like a doddery old uncle and just get rid of some of this awful unreality. His shit was flying out all over the place.

Frank looked only a little surprised when Damien entered his office. He made him a cup of rosehip tea and sat, smiling sadly. Damien looked at the row upon row of books to the ceiling. Nietzsche and Schopenhauer. Joyce. Shakespeare. Some poetry, but mostly old Latin and Greek crap. And I bet he's read them all, he thought.

"I have indeed," said Frank.

"What?"

"Read them all. Some are due for re-reading. I've always thought re-reading is even better than the first time, because there's also the pleasure of anticipation, like waiting for someone you love to appear, as opposed to a stranger."

"But how did you know what I was thinking?" asked Damien.

"Some faces are easy to read. Transparent almost. The passage of thought from the brain to those muscles which control the facial architecture is direct and almost ludicrous in its simplicity."

Was he insulting him? Deliberately insulting him? Had he really just said what he thought he'd said? The old fool was looking in a troubled way at a few sheets of paper headed *PhD PROPOSAL*. Was this old twat some sort of mind freak? The whole world was beginning to feel unstable. Damien decided to ignore the mind reading insult. Best to stay with simple facts for now.

"I've just been to see Professor Trevalyan about getting a proper salary," he said.

"Dear boy, I hope you didn't ask him to pay you what you're worth. Nobody could live on that," Frank said with a cheerful but faraway smile.

Now Damien looked, he could see that Frank's pupils were definitely dilated. Perhaps he was a geriatric crackhead or something.

"Frank, I was hoping for a bit of solidarity. Workers uniting. Soldiers together. Brothers in Arms, as Mark Knopfler said."

"Indeed. Soon we'll all be uniting. Academics, murderers, tyrants. Doubtless the floodgates will open. Now shrills the trump its dire alarms: At once the warriors cry to arms: Heaven thunders back the note. Book Nine. Dear boy, shall you and I alone hope to break the shielded foe?"

"Right," said Damien. "And what are you on exactly, Frank?"

"I am on the ocean blown, or tossed on shore from stone to stone. Anger and shame should overpower fear, but alas ..." he made a gesture of dismissal.

Damien left. The old tosser was clearly having a bad reality day. Frank looked up. Surely someone had been there a moment ago, talking about how they must fight the arrival of General Spinelli together. He hoped he hadn't said anything untoward. He'd noticed several things about the painkillers recently: a tendency to say just what he was thinking, which experience had taught him was invariably a mistake, and an occasional and unpredictable flash of awareness of what certain people, usually the less bright, were thinking. Nevertheless, the painkillers did provide a buffer against the encroaching awfulness of reality. He took another. He noticed a pink folder entitled POEMS on a chair. Someone must have been here. Yes, he remembered now, it was the Creative Writing person. Frank opened the folder and started to read.

Chapter Twelve

Trevor tried another list:

> REASONS WHY CYNTH MIGHT REJECT ME
> Spotty
> Tendency to flush
> Sweats a lot
> No friends

That would do for now. No point in labouring his deficiencies. Confidence was a fragile thing. He wrote another list:

> REASONS WHY CYNTH MIGHT LOVE ME
> Intriguing loner
> Great writer
> Excellent lover
> Attentive listener

He bluetacked them on the wall. Four things in each list, so no outright winner, and "Intriguing loner" was the flip side of "No friends", which suggested that you could look at the same quality in different ways, and ambivalence was a crucial attribute in a writer. But how might She Who is Adored look at it? That was what he needed to do – know exactly what she thought, and how could he do that? Another list was called for:

> POSSIBLE THOUGHTS OF CYNTH ON TREV:
> He's a loser
> He would be devoted to me
> He seems to flush and sweat a lot
> He's passionate

Spots on forehead
He's read a lot
Fantastic orgasms
He's a tosser
We could talk about writing
Doesn't smell

No, it was no good; it was all over the place. He needed to boil it down into two lists: POSITIVE AND NEGATIVE THOUGHTS ABOUT TREV. Perhaps another list was called for too: FEELINGS AS WELL AS THOUGHTS; that way he might dream up some interesting metaphors and similes about her state of mind and heart, and later, when they were lying in bed together in postcoital ecstasy, he could share them with her. This sort of creative list would have the added benefit of helping him to be a great writer. However, there was a further problem; suppose the first time they went to bed together he was so nervous he couldn't get an erection? First fucks were notoriously fraught and could be disastrous, so he made a quick list of possible strategies:

STRATEGIES FOR GETTING A STIFFY
Go to the bathroom and work on it
Make a joke about it (The jocular lightening of intensity would ensure an erection)
Ask her for assistance
Get Viagra (Where? The doctor's? The Student Counsellor? The Asian Grocer's at home?)
Say I've been ill and try next time
Kill myself
Concentrate on writing and forget about sex

OK, now we're getting somewhere, he thought. Then realised he didn't have a clue where he was. Each list appeared to take him closer to the object of his desires, but then numerous other technical problems swam into his mind to distance her, problems that had to be considered before he could attempt a full frontal assault. Important things had to be established, such as what kind of kissing she liked.

He made a list, which included: *long and lingering; brief but ecstatic; brief but full of promise; rapid little pecky budgie kisses; butterfly kisses; juicy and wet.* Each had its own virtue, but its own danger too: *juicy and wet*, for example, could easily slide from something voluptuous to drooling up a ton of spit like some weird giant insect stuck to your lips. *Invasion of the Insect Snoggers.* Actually, there might be a novel or screenplay in that, with the insects as a sort of metaphor for destructive love.

He practised the various sorts of kiss on the back of his hand, the way he'd seen his little sister do, then against the mirror, and finally decided on a distillation of *brief but ecstatic* and *juicy and wet*, a sort of *brief but juicy* frisson. He wrote down *brief but juicy* on a scrap of paper and put it in his pocket.

It was always possible that he might meet her unexpectedly in a leafy glade, the glorious moment would arrive and he'd need a few helpful prompts. He decided that once he had enough lists, he would try to distil them into headings on mini Post-its and secrete them about his body. That might create difficulties once he was bone naked, but he'd cross that bridge once he came to it. Not only was love a problem, it was one which became increasingly complex the longer one travelled into it.

Cynth went back to her room in a mood of absorbed self-examination. The kiss in the lift had been forceful and unexpected. Her lips tingled and she could taste Damien; a potpourri of heavy aftershave and blackberry lip balm. She looked at her slightly bruised mouth in the mirror.

She ran through the possibilities: He was secretly in love with her. She didn't think so, not with She Who Is Infinitely Unlovable. He mistook her for someone else? Given her size, this was highly unlikely unless he had suddenly gone totally blind. He did it for a bet or a dare, like the boy with Bessie Bighead in *Under Milk Wood.* No, he wasn't the type, and in any case, how would he prove he'd done it since no one saw and he jumped away the moment the lift doors opened? Perhaps he was overcome with abstract lust and she just happened to be there. She understood being overcome with a desire for something (the dreaded tin and Ely Cathedral always waiting provocatively), but she knew instinctively this wasn't the case.

Dad had said to her once that men used the idea of ungovernable passions simply to justify doing what the hell they felt like doing. She would have asked him about this if he hadn't deserted her and left her with this, and all other problems; the tin, the abyss beyond. Just thinking about Dad made her heart physically ache.

She sat at her little desk, feeling both the ache and the fact of the kiss. A kiss was a strange thing, the mouth seeking something other than food or air, offering something other than words or exclamations. The mouth seeking something for itself. The mouth wishing to stop the possibility of language. The mouth's song to itself. The curious thing about the kiss, she realised with astonishing clarity, was that it meant so little to her. Compared to the ache it was nothing. She had been kissed by a poet, the Creative Writing Director, whom some of the First year girls clearly fancied like mad. She'd overheard two of them talking about his reputation. Yet it meant so little to her. She felt neither flattered nor chosen. She would remember it, but the way one remembers herpes or a heavy cold. She also had a sense that what Damien most desired was himself.

She had given him her poems because she felt something was required in exchange, but now she wanted them back. She didn't want them read by anyone, not yet, not until she felt ready. She would have to retrieve them. The problem would be talking. She knew that once she got to Damien's office she'd find it hard to say anything, as she always did, but especially now after the kiss, even if it did mean so little.

Talking to people was such a problem. That's why she'd stopped. No one noticed.

Chapter Thirteen

Damien had found relief, or was in the process of finding it, between the somewhat creaky thighs of Mercedes Blonk. She was looking for a diversion and saw him come out of Frank's office looking bewildered and troubled. A Channel Four interview had been cancelled, which meant she had the rest of the day to kill and she had no intention of wasting it on work.

She had almost decided against having Damien as he was no challenge, and there would not be the quiver of delight she always experienced with First Year boys, the bubble of excitement that went with fresh meat. Her instincts had proven right. She was spread-eagled on her desk, face down, and he was inside her from behind, still wearing the frilly shirt, his trousers ballooning around his ankles. He was muttering away, but apparently to himself: "Yes, yes, go on, go on then, boy. Come on, boy."

"For God's sake, try a bit of variety," she said. "Faster, slower, anything."

"Yes, yes, faster, slower," muttered Damien, pulling in and out at exactly the same pace.

She found herself face to face with a copy of her book, *The Pudenda Chronicles.* The photograph of her on the front was a good one, taken ten years ago, wearing a lime green boob tube and heavy mascara. Ten years had aged her but she still got by on charisma and reputation.

She had been with Tony then, among others. He was a good man, lively, funny. She could have had a child with him. He wanted to and she knew that it was probably her last biological chance, but she'd just been offered the BBC Late Night Review and, frankly, it was no conflict. Yet now, facing her younger self, she wondered which would really have been the most interesting life. She and Tony would doubtless have split, but she would have a *someone*, a child, who needed her constantly, for whom she had to be there and who would be there for her.

Unfairly, now it was too late, it seemed like a good thing. Perhaps the possibility was all the sweeter because it was out of the question. After all, if she didn't know what a tricky thing the subconscious was, then who did? But there would have been the daily fact of another life to be considered, the bittersweet challenge of a blood tie. And now, somehow, during the intervening years, unquestioning love had stopped being a possibility. She wondered if there had been an exact moment. Then she head-butted the book off the desk as Damien speeded up.

"Yes, yes, come on boy!" And he whooped himself to a climax, ending in the self-exultation of "Damien! Damien!"

And how was it for me? She wondered, as Damien collapsed in a sweaty heap on her back, twitching slightly. She definitely preferred First Years.

Relief was starting to play on Brimley's mind too. Things had definitely got blocked in the system again. Once CRAP really got going and the staff cull was given a green light, he could sack someone every few days, thereby ensuring a scintillating bowel movement at least twice a week for three months, which would be the closest thing to heaven he could imagine. For now, he needed something else. He'd had three mugs of coffee and tried a glycerin suppository, but that was like trying to bulldoze through a church with a Tonka toy. Nora came in and immediately intuited the situation.

"Nothing?" she asked, looking at him like a sympathetic nurse.

"Not a squit, Nora."

"We might have to consider something a little more radical," she said.

"Like what?"

"My friend Margaret is a colonic irrigationist."

"Absolutely not. I'm not having some strange woman ramming a garden hose up my anus." Brimley felt his bowels shrink at the thought.

"She'd do special rates, seeing as you and I … you know …"

"She can take her special rates and … and keep them. But thanks for the thought, Nora. It's refreshing to know you think of my … er … welfare."

"My pleasure," Nora assured him. "Have you had any luck with the other thing?"

"What thing?" Brimley, wondered to what other part of his physiognomy she was referring.

"The weekend, silly."

Shit. Why oh why? He'd forgotten. He had told Nora he'd take her to a B&B somewhere for the weekend and tell his wife he was at a conference, but he'd forgotten. Nora tended to desert his thoughts as soon as she was out of sight, and sometimes even before that. However, it was convenient having her there, and occasionally having her; secretaries were much more willing to do that little bit more, go the next mile, stay on that extra hour, if you were having an affair with them. He considered it was convenient all round, as she lived with her aged mother and couldn't get out much. The odd night with Brimley was just about all the fun she had.

"I'm sorry. Really sorry, but it's the kids. Helen's going off somewhere, you know how selfish she can be, and I'm lumbered with them. We'll do it soon. Promise."

She smiled and hid her disappointment, took his empty coffee mug and left. He didn't know the great lengths she'd gone to arranging for her mother to be looked after this weekend. And he probably wouldn't care if he did. He'd just promised they'd go away soon, so there was an end to it. She might take Mum out in her wheelchair to the common if the weather was fine.

Meanwhile, there were memos to type, course outlines to distribute and booklists to update. There was a lot to do.

Chapter Fourteen

Damien was enjoying a post coital glow, which restored his self esteem. He was in his study dispensing nuggets of wisdom to Helen. If he hadn't so recently chopped his liver with Mercedes he might have made a play for her there and then, but all things would come. A little patience sometimes enhanced their sweetness, just as he would revel in his assured literary fame all the more because it had been denied him for too long. Jesus, Shelley had been dead for seven years by the time he was my age, he thought.

"Your work has promise," he said. "You can tell a story alright, but you need a little more experience to give you that something, that authority, that will improve it. Technique plus experience equals good writing."

"Aye, but what sort of experience?" asked Helen.

A number of things came into Damien's mind, which he couldn't possibly say just yet.

"Just live, go with what you feel. Experiment. Try new things."

"You mean hang gliding an' that? Or going on a kibbutz or something?"

That was not what he meant. Was she thick or what? There was a knock at the door.

"Come," said Damien.

The door opened and the fat thing stood there. What the hell did she want? Oh Christ, she mustn't say anything about the incident that didn't happen in the lift. Damien shot up from his seat and went to the door so that if the fat thing said anything Helen wouldn't hear. She just stood staring at him, her chubby cheeks flushed.

Oh God, she was in love with him. She was going to start pursuing him, writing him notes, e-mailing him, telephoning. She might even be one of those who started contacting him at home;

55

then he'd have a row with his wife and have to convince her that he was the victim here, the stalked, and he needed sympathy, and his wife would apologise and things would eventually get back to normal, but after a lot of unnecessary fuss. Why was life so complicated and unfair?

"What is it, er …?" He realised he didn't even know her name. If he got it wrong, she might get hysterical and start crying or shouting. Women were so unpredictable and unreasonable. Her lips were slightly bruised. He could sense Helen looking at them both.

"Listen. Could we talk later?" he hissed.

She just stared.

"I'm busy now."

And she stared on. Damien glanced over his shoulder and could see Helen was watching intently. He had to get rid of the fat thing before Helen started to suspect. He'd planned to write another great poem later, but literature and immortality would have to wait.

"Could you come back in an hour?"

She stared more. Something stirred in Damien's mind. The word "poem" had done it. What was it? Yes! The fat thing had given him her bloody poems. That's why she was here – not only to force herself upon him but also to get quick feedback on her sodding work. She obviously thought he would be panting at the leash to read them. Honestly, students were so selfish, so self obsessed. Not only was she in love with him, but she expected him to offer insights into her poetry as well.

"Your poems. Is that it?"

The fat thing nodded. Damien looked back at Helen.

"She wants her poems," he said, as if it explained everything. But where were the bloody things? They weren't on his desk.

"I'll get them back for you by Monday. Haven't had time to give them the attention they deserve. Alright?" And he closed the door. This was becoming a day he'd be glad to see the back of, despite the interlude with Mercedes, but even she had seemed slightly remote after their coupling. He'd probably taken her breath away. It happened.

Chapter Fifteen

Trevor was in turmoil. His room was now wallpapered with lists, but, rather than clarify, they seemed to confuse. They were shopping lists of possibilities and each item demanded a list of its own, multiplying and breeding until he had started to make lists of the lists of the lists.

They should have distilled his love into orderly plans and strategies. His campaign to win Cynth should by now have been rationalised down to the tiniest detail. He should be clear, strong and single-minded. But instead he felt as if his mind was in danger of exploding into a thousand pieces, with painful thoughts wriggling on their points like fish in agony. His love had become a vast, thrashing ocean. Suddenly it all seemed too much. He didn't feel up to the task of wooing and winning Cynth. He lacked confidence and experience and was aware that the former probably came as a result of the latter. There was only one solution ...

An hour later, as it grew dark, Trevor Bottom was on the bus away from campus. He'd decided to go in disguise, just in case any tutors or students were around, so he'd thickened his usually light brown and wispy eyebrows with a black felt tip then toned it down with some red, giving him the appearance of an emaciated and startled ginger owl. He brushed his hair over his forehead and tinted that black. He also wore a pink bobble hat knitted by his well meaning but completely batty gran, who had always believed Trevor was a girl, and a scarf around his mouth. He'd heard of the Moleshill Road, the red light area of the city, and assumed it would be easy to find.

The bus cruised around the ring road, the supermarkets and bowling alleys and malls giving way to thinner, darker streets where every other shop seemed to be selling kebabs, and between them *Prakash Quality Clothing, Guptar Indian Takeaway, Wills and Son Second Hand Furniture, Dyson's Exchange Shop* and *Bridie's Off License,* behind metal grilles thick enough to stop a tank. It got darker. A lot of people seemed to be standing watching the bus or passing cars or each other or nothing in particular, and mostly in huddled little groups, pin points of red where their cigarettes glowed. The bus stopped, scattering one of the small mountains of rubbish in the kerb.

"Is this the Moleshill Road?" Trev asked the driver.

"Wha' you think iss; fuckin' Bloomsbury, mate?"

He was doing this for Cynth. He mustn't back out now. He got off and immediately two huge black figures stood either side of him. Trev looked at the retreating bus, wishing to heaven he'd stayed on it.

"You wan' ganja, my man?"

Ganja? What the hell was that? Some sort of drug, or weird sex, or time share?

"No thanks," said Trev.

"Yeah you do, you wan' ganja," the figure persisted.

Trev could see one of the teeth was missing in the luminous white smile framed by dreadlocks.

"No, I really don't want any ganja," Trev said.

"Oh yeah, you want this fine ganja. Moroccan. Very cool. I give you a good deal 'cos we're friends. We got a good intimacy thing here."

"Honestly, I don't want any," said Trev, worried about the assumption of intimacy that seemed to have arrived with alarming speed and without his permission.

"How much you wan', then?"

"I don't want any. I'm sorry."

"A half ounce. Or I give you some good blow," said the figure.

"I don't want you to give me a good blow, but thanks for offering," said Trev.

"Sure you want. How much in your pocket? I give you excellent blow."

"I just want to go away," said Trev, feeling tears pricking the rims of his eyes. It was like being back at school, in the playground, with some psycho killer hiding in a ten-year-old child's body and threatening you. He comforted himself with the thought that it would be useful material for his writing, assuming he got out of here alive.

"You don't want? Then why the big fuck you wastin' my time? Why you stop me and my brother here for? Time is money, my man."

"I didn't stop you. You were just sort of there," said Trevor, knowing he'd made a colossal mistake in coming into this dark, hostile, urban war zone.

"I'm here, Captain Sensible, 'cos this is my patch. Question is – why's you here if you don't wanna buy?" The tone had changed to *I'm about to put you in hospital if you don't do what I want.*

To Trev's immense relief, a police car cruised by and he took the opportunity to run for his life. After a few hundred yards he realised he was running the wrong way – actually further into this heart of darkness, where shadows watched you suspiciously, where people wanted you to buy their ganja and then blow you. He wished he was in his room making a list and quietly, but safely, going mad with love.

"Don't worry," said a female voice.

He looked around and from a doorway a young woman came into view. She was smiling, had long dark hair, long dark boots on her long dark legs and a skirt the width of Scotch Tape. A little tight leather jacket covered what novels often called "ample breasts."

"You in need of relief? You look all hot and sweaty," she said kindly.

"Are you a prostitute?" Trevor asked, emboldened by the adrenalin rush of his recent terror.

"Do you want one?" she asked, unfazed.

"I did, but now I'm wondering if I should just get out of here."

"I know a place where we can be quiet for a while. You can catch your breath, recover. Then I'll get you a cab if you like."

"Are you offering to take me to a room where we can have full sexual intercourse?'"

"If that's what you'd like," she said.

"How much will it cost?"

"How much have you got?"

"Forty five pounds."

"That's how much it costs."

Trevor took the notes from his wallet and offered them.

"No. Pay him," she said.

Trevor turned around and a large figure stood before him, grinning, one tooth missing in the luminous dreadlock-framed smile. Shit. His nemesis again. The man took the money.

"Thankin' you, my man. I knew we could do business," he said, the smile broadening. "You should ha' tol' me you wanted to shake the snake with a bitch. We coulda got here much quicker."

The girl led him away into an alley. He felt powerless, dream-like. He was going to do it. He was going to become a man for Cynth, so that he could win her with confidence and strength. This was a necessary step, like going to war for democracy and freedom. He was a soldier about to go over the top and through the ramparts.

Her name was Sonia, she told him, as she led him up some creaky stairs and into a small room with a single overhead light. Incongruously there was a Deputy Dawg poster on one wall and a picture of Winston Churchill smiling ruefully and giving a two-fingered V for Victory sign. A single bed, with a roll of paper towel at the bottom. Sonia filled a bowl of water from a dingy sink.

"Let's clean you up, baby," she said.

"But I am clean," said Trev. "I had a shower this morning and two baths before I came out, when I'd decided to … you know."

"Sure, but I have to check you out anyway," she said, smiling.

"Can't I check myself out?"

"You're not getting the point. I have to see you're OK. Not infected or anything. Don't worry. It'll all be nice. Sweet and soapy."

Oh my God, oh my dearheart, Hail Mary Jesus, she was going

to touch him and wash his bits in that little tin bowl. She undid his jeans and they slipped to the floor. He felt the sweat start to leak from his forehead and into his eyes. He also felt his manhood shrivel protectively into his Luke Skywalker boxers.

"Can't we talk for a bit first?"

She didn't answer. She was looking at him, horrified, as she dropped the bowl and backed away. What was wrong? He'd only suggested a bit of a chat.

"All I asked was …"

But she backed away further as he shuffled towards her, hampered by the jeans around his ankles.

"You get away!" she yelled. "Whatever's wrong with you I don't want it."

What the hell was she talking about? He was the one who should be worried about infection and disease. Then he caught sight of himself in a mirror above the sink and recoiled. His head was leaking all down his face. Dark, thick liquid that dripped onto his coat. He looked terrifying. How could he not have felt pain with all that bloody gore coming from him?

The door suddenly opened and the gap-toothed one entered the room.

"You all right, Sonia, babe? This mutha hurt you? What the …?" as he looked at the state of Trevor's face.

As Trev was being dragged downstairs by his new friend, he realised it was the felt tips he'd used to colour his eyebrows and hair that had run with sweat, but it seemed useless to try to explain this as his head bumped from stair to stair. He felt dazed as he was dumped in the street and his friend went through his pockets, took his wallet and keys, and went back inside. With a gulp of misery, Trev looked down at his thin legs. His jeans had come off as he was being dragged downstairs but it didn't seem wise to go back for them.

An hour and a half later, gone midnight and after a horrendous journey, dodging in and out of shadows, to get back to the university unseen, Trev was trying to climb a drainpipe to get in his room, his keys having been stolen. His Luke Skywalker boxers got caught in a loose screw and flicked off with a ping. Moments later, a strong torch beam illuminated his pale buttocks.

Moments after that the security guard had him in an armlock and marched him to the security office, where another guard, with a beer belly straining his Bittermouth Blue shirt, was eating a cheeseburger.

"Found this perv trying to climb in a back winder," said the first guard. "Sez 'e's a student so I sez why you bollock naked then and got all that crap on your head and face 'e sez 'e don't know, 'ad a blackout or summink. Likely fuckin' story I sez. What shall I do wiv 'im, Baz?"

Baz gave a little cheesy belch.

"You'd better search him. Might be on drugs or something."

"I ain't doin' a full body no way. I got no rubber gloves. Missus took 'em for the garden," said the first guard.

Baz sniffed.

"Reckon you're a student, do you?"

"Yes," said Trev. "Honest. Trevor Bottom; Bottom of the First year."

Baz smirked. "Bottom, eh? How apt. Well, Mr Bottom, if you're really a student tell me something I don't know."

"What?" asked Trev.

"I don't know what, that's why I'm asking. Enlighten me. Feed me a morsel of knowledge. Titillate me with a revelatory fact. Challenge my frontal lobes with a ground-breaking theory. Don't be shy, Mr Bottom. You're a clever fucking bastard, so you said, or were you lying through your tits?"

"I didn't say I was clever. I just said I was a student." Trev had a sickening, lumpy feeling that this would get worse before it got better.

"Oh, pedantic tosser, are you, eh? Right. Let's examine this then: You're implying that to be a student you should be pig-fucking ignorant with nothing to say about anything. Now, correct me if I'm wrong, but the people who go to university – unlike me who has do a shit number like security because my parents couldn't afford to keep me on at school – I say students are meant to be the crème de la crème, the icing on the cake, the top ten percent, the roses growing out of the horse shit, are they not, my little knobbly-kneed Einstein?"

"I just want to get into my room and go to sleep," said Trev.

"I reckon they should castrate rapists, just give 'em the chop, see 'ow they like that. Can't do no damage with a stump. Bleedin' pervs can't," said the first guard.

Baz eyed Trev suspiciously.

"I'm going to let you go this time because, despite going to the school of hard knocks and having my juvenile aspirations to be a molecular biologist crushed like so many spring daisies under the jackboot of life, I still retain a charitable disposition. Difficult to believe, but it's true. So you can go, and Dave here will let you in with his master key.

"First, just for our files and occasional amusement, I have to keep a visual record of this highly improbable incident. Our records are second to none, our diligence held in awe by no less than the Chancellor himself, who gained a First Class Honours in Classics at Cambridge," said Baz, with another cheesy belch.

Trev stood there, looking over his shoulder and into the lens while Baz took a back-view Polaroid of his naked, humiliated misery.

Ten minutes later he collapsed on his bed, then had a shower and decided that the only way to blot out the sheer horror of the evening was to make a very long list of all that had happened, then file it away as research for a future novel, which he would definitely write in the third person.

Chapter Sixteen

After a night of excruciating dreams in which he was variously minced, diced and castrated by a giant set of dentures with a gap in the centre, Trevor knew he had to act decisively. His own attempts at understanding and directing his passion for Cynth had so far taken him to the frontiers of sanity, nearly got him beaten to a pulp, his wallet and keys stolen, and humiliated him in front of an arsey security guard, and cost him forty-five quid. He had also been terrified of Sonia touching him, and rather than gaining a magnificent erection at the thought, he had shrivelled into a miniature Parisienne carrot.

Perhaps there was something physically wrong with him. Suppose Cynth fell for him only to discover that he had a cruel affliction that meant every time he should get an erection he actually got a shrivel instead? He knew he was capable of getting one because he whacked off at last once a day, but that was just with himself, a few tissues, some hand cream and his imagination. Perhaps that was the root of the problem, so to speak. He'd become a sort of amoeba that could only mate with itself, or by binary fission.

He would have to test whether or not he could get an erection in public, but how could he do that? He couldn't just walk into a bank or a supermarket, drop his pants and start rubbing up. Christ, it was a nightmare. He needed professional help. He decided to skip Damien's Creative Writing workshop – Writing through your Senses – and headed for the medical centre.

Dr Duff was an unusual choice for the job because he had an aversion to sick people. In fact he hated them. The very idea of illness made him ill.

The Registrar had thought it a cunning appointment, because

students and malingering staff soon stopped going to Duff, and that made running the university more efficient. At least until it gained its own pharmaceutical department, at which time they could corner the market in prescribed drugs on campus and everyone could be sick as often as they liked. But by then the master plan, the Final Solution, would be in place anyway and students would be a thing of the past.

Trevor shifted uncomfortably in the seat opposite Dr Duff, who wore a surgical mask and eyed him suspiciously.

"Is there an epidemic or something on campus?" Trevor asked.

"What?" asked Duff, horrified. "An epidemic! My God, what have you heard?"

"Nothing. It's just the mask …"

"Oh. I always wear the mask. Only …" he looked around warily, "I get a lot of sick people in here. You wouldn't believe how they just barge in coughing and spreading their germs around. I have to be careful. And a lot of them want me to examine them as well. Touch their diseased bodies. It's scary. Do you play tennis?"

"What? No, no, I'm not very good at sports," said Trev.

"Only I need a doubles partner. You should take up tennis. Gets you out in the air, away from diseases and people sneezing all over you. Have you any idea how many new bacteria you've introduced into this surgery?"

"How many?"

"Twenty-four million. And that's a conservative estimate. It doesn't even include the deadly ones. Look at this little fellow." The doctor switched on an overhead projector and, on the wall to the right, appeared something that might have been an arthritic centipede.

"Salmonella typhi. Gives you typhoid fever. And this Jezebel …" Here a slide of wavy lines in a roughish circle. "Vibrio cholera, classic cholera."

A new slide showed what could have been miniscule octopi. "And these little bastards, azotobacter, will get right in, feed on your organic materials and give you inflammation of whatever they damn well choose. Nasty, eh? But there's more …"

Another slide of what looked like countless eyes.

"Innocent looking, eh? But don't be deceived, my friend. Pneumonia." Another slide of what looked like kidney beans with holes. "Bacillus anthracis. These dirty little soldiers will give you anthrax soon as look at you."

The good doctor looked at Trevor.

"So don't tell me your walking into my surgery is an innocent event, because I have the scientific proof that shows otherwise. Don't ever mention to me azotobacter or bacillus radicocola, life enhancing nitrogenous compounds, because I will look you in the eye and say coccus and spirillum.

"People come in here to destroy me. And do they apologise? Do they hell. They are walking colonies of disease, continents of death. Even as I look at you now, how can I think anything other than streptococcus pyogenes?"

The doctor leaned back, exhausted by his catalogue of potential death.

"Can I tell you why I'm here?" asked Trevor.

The doctor considered for a moment then spoke reluctantly. "All right then. If you must. What seems to be the problem?"

Trevor blushed scarlet and his face turned damp and waxy. Dr Duff thought he might have some sort of plague and pushed his chair back a little. He took a can from a drawer and sprayed the room with something antiseptic smelling then he opened the window further and took a few breaths of air from outside.

"It's, it's … it's just … It's …"

"It's some sort of speech problem, is it? A stutter by the sound of it. You should try singing. Interesting thing; people don't stutter when they sing."

"It's not a speech problem. It's just … I'm not sure if I can get an erection when I'm in front of a woman."

"What do you mean, in front?"

"I just mean with her."

"And why do you want to be with a woman?"

"Because … because I'm a bloke. It's what we do."

"So if everyone else put their heads in a gas oven, you would too, eh?" The doctor nodded as if he'd just proven his case.

"No. But it's natural to want to do it with a woman," persisted Trev.

"Is it indeed? And are you married?"

"No."

"That's the answer, then. If you're not married, you shouldn't be thinking about sex in any case. And even then, you should proceed only with extreme caution. Do you know how many germs and bacteria and wotnot are exchanged genitally during what is laughingly referred to as the act of love?"

"No, how many?"

"Well, I don't know exactly … but a hell of a lot, I can tell you. Enough to give you a nasty dose of something or other," said the doctor, taken aback, wondering if his grasp of facts was slipping and if this signified the immediate onset of dementia.

"You think exchanging bodily fluids comes without dire consequences? Ha! Penetrative violation, or love as some fools choose to call it, causes more deaths on this planet than anything else."

"Doesn't it also cause a lot of life? I mean babies and stuff," said Trev.

"Babies. Don't mention babies to me. Puking and soiling themselves wherever they go. And for what? They are born into a world of pain, infections and disease so miniscule that the infants don't even know they are playing host to millions of tiny deaths. Ischemia, ulcers, diphtheria, hyperthyroidism, melanoma, ataxia. They're all going to die, so what have they got to gurgle about? Maybe they know. Maybe that's why they cry so much. Good God, I know I do. I'm a doctor, I understand these things. And look …"

Another slide of wavy lines. "Spirochaetes. These little dirty darlings will give you syphilis. The shakes, memory loss, trembling, nervous collapse, muscular deterioration. The whole human structure breaks down at a primary cellular and molecular level. A horrible, horrible death that even a god who hates the human race wouldn't wish upon us. So, for pity's sake, stop thinking about sex and take an aspirin.

"Are you sure about the tennis? Look as though you might have a useful backhand."

Chapter Seventeen

Damien was enjoying himself. He felt back in control. The students were all lying on their backs with their eyes closed. The lights were off and the room was in shadow. He could see with some satisfaction that Helen's breasts protruded enticingly. Fresh twin peaks. He decided he'd invite her for another personal tutorial tomorrow and have a bottle of wine chilling in the common room. They would sip it before and after they'd made love on this very floor.

He might read her some of his poems from what he saw as his 'rage period'. He thought of the reviews those earlier works would generate once he was firmly established as the brightest star in the literary firmament: "fierce poems that perfectly capture a young man's anger against the world's injustices … images as sharp as daggers … the sentiments of a brave heart … postmodernity at its most perfectly executed … language in the hands of a master craftsman …"

He was drifting again. The students were dutifully lying there like corpses. How long since he'd said anything? What the hell did he last say anyway? Something about sun and warmth. Yes, that was it; Writing Through Your Senses. On a beach on a desert island.

"Keep your eyes closed. Good. Deep breaths. Slowly in and out. Relax. Feel your pores open, your muscles relax. It's warm, you're on a beach, there's no one else around, which is why you've taken off all your clothes and can feel the sun kissing your nakedness. It's good."

He stepped over the fat thing that seemed to be taking up most of the room, wondering why the hell he'd kissed her and where the hell were her sodding poems. He stood beside Helen, so that she would feel his nearness, the undulating cadences of his voice, and know he was speaking specifically to her.

"A stranger approaches. You feel his presence even before you open your eyes. Then you look up and see his outline against the sun. Even though he is in shadow, you can feel his smile. You know this is a beginning, something is going to happen, something sensual. And you know that the world of sensations is a force bigger than yourself, especially now that your senses are keen, heightened ..."

He stopped abruptly, stunned, shocked. He could not believe it. Someone had snored. A sort of snorty snore as they started to doze off and suddenly woke up again. Someone had the audacity to nod off and snore during his Writing Through Your Senses workshop. He was sure it was the fat thing. How dare she be bored? He glared at her. Bitch. She could wait for her bloody poems, even if he did find them. She probably did it on purpose to gain his attention, to connect with him, to persist in the illusion that they were involved in a relationship. God, the cheek, the sheer fucking audacity.

Cynth had been naked on the beach, but the sun made her drowsy, and Damien's voice started to sound like the tide, swelling and falling monotonously. To spice up her imagining she visualised a hamper full of chocolate and started on a Cadbury Flake, which had half melted in the heat, but she ate it anyway and then coaxed a liquid Twix from its gold wrapper. She was enjoying it so much she could actually taste the chocolate in her mouth, hear the waves a long way off, feel the sun pinking her skin. Then she felt the sun go behind a cloud, which was odd because the sky had been spectacularly clear.

She opened her eyes and a shadowed figure was standing over her. Guiltily she dropped the Twix in the sand and was acutely aware of the smeared chocolate on her hands and around her lips. This mattered more than her nakedness. Even though he was only an outline, it was someone she knew better than herself, and she also knew with a killing certainty that he would have that gentle, bewildered expression on his face that he always wore when she did something to pain him. She was his little girl, his baby, and he'd caught her pigging out on the beach. He shook his head sadly.

She wanted to say something to change everything, but no words came and the chocolate taste in her mouth soured.

The ache settled deep in her heart again and the sting of tears made her blink in the semi-darkness. Why had he come then? Why not before she started on the chocolate? Why did the timing of things always betray her? The ache was deep inside her now, an immense longing and knowledge that the big things could never be put right. If only she could choose a moment in the past when he had been there and loved her, she would relinquish all else – all experiences, all possibilities – to live in that moment forever, with him. The ache grew and seemed bigger than even her, to engulf her. And from far inside it all life was reduced to a single sob, which she tried to stifle, unsuccessfully.

To Damien, however, it was a snore, and he was bitterly offended. He gave these students so much, and all they could do in return was snort like pigs.

Chapter Eighteen

Trevor Bottom was feeling more desperate than ever. He walked past the Tower of Light, blinded by the reflections from the window. He went to the library and sought out a section on romance.

He didn't want some self-help crap, like his older sister read. He'd tried getting experience in the heart of darkness and it hadn't worked, so now he wanted wisdom, a helpful way of looking at love and the world, an idea to anchor him, something that linked heart and mind so that he could enjoy his love without going barking mad. He'd done a trawl through the Internet but it just took him to pay per view porn sites. Of all the millions of books in the world, there must be one that could help. Then, one day, when he and Cynth were living in sexual bliss, with two Yorkshire terriers and a house by the sea, he could write a book about this turbulent period of his life and offer his own wisdom to others.

He looked along the shelves. God, it was confusing: *Romantic Affinities*, *Romance and Sexuality*, *Gendering Romanticism*, *Romantic Tradition*, *Rhetoric of Romanticism*, *Romantic Image*, *Romanticism and Social Change: A Structural Analysis of Romance*. Hundreds and hundreds of them, row upon row, and each referring to yet more. Both he and Cynth would be dead before he got through this lot.

He was a fast and clever reader, but now he was in a state and his concentration had exploded. He needed a quick fix, not a five-year homeopathic plan. He closed his eyes, ran a thin finger along the shelves and let providence guide him. He stopped when he felt the moment was right, opened his eyes and took down the book: *The Romantic Disposition*. An old book, little borrowed. He opened it at random and started reading. After a few minutes he found it:

> *In the Romantic disposition, love fragments in order to re-combine, dissolves to reassemble, changes to increase. Love is the Dark Angel who takes us into unknown territories of the heart, and waits to hear what we find there.*

That was what he needed. He liked the bit about things having to fall apart in order to come together – falling horribly apart had certainly been his experience so far. This book seemed to be suggesting that all that confusion was *necessary* because he was in unknown territories of the heart, and the Dark Angel was waiting to hear about his torment, and once he'd told him, he'd be free. Brilliant.

Obviously there wasn't a real Dark Angel, but there might be a someone, a special person, a mentoring shaman, a high priest of love. It was comforting to think this was the case. After all, a sort of random providence had led him to this particular book. Perhaps higher powers really were at work.

He looked at who had written the book. Frank Finch. The name was familiar. Yes, he was in the English department. It was a miracle! The writer of *The Romantic Disposition* was actually in this university. Perhaps Frank could be Trevor's own Dark Angel and listen solemnly to his story. He felt a great weight lift from his mind, and the fist that had started to squeeze his heart unclenched. Perhaps he also heard the faint rustling of wings. He would go to his angel and learn the truth of things.

The poems were astonishingly good. Raw, in need of editing, but they had a structural soundness and an emotional power that was undeniable.

Frank read them twice, the second time because he thought that perhaps the painkillers had numbed his critical faculties. But the poems had, if anything, gained in subtlety and power on further scrutiny. They had even distracted him from the pipes, which had been playing Debussy's *La Mer* at such a heart-attacking pace that Frank started to hyperventilate, until he took another two painkillers and the poems exerted their imaginative hold.

Many in the form of dramatic monologue were addressed to someone older, certainly male, a strange sort of shadowy father figure that the poetic voice was struggling both with and against. It was this combative engagement of language, the painful journey to be articulate and honest, the muscling of lines against each other, that gave the poems an exquisite tension.

They were by somebody called C. Blake. Well, thought Frank, if the Creative Writing chap was getting this sort of work from students, he would have to revise his idea of the young man, and of Creative Writing, which he had always thought a rather ludicrous notion – that one could do a degree in it. A production line of would-be writers. A giant battery farm of literary chicks. He put the poems in an internal post envelope with a note to Damien.

There was a knock at the door. It opened and a strange, disturbed looking young man entered. He was thin and spotty with inflamed eyes. Frank had another momentary and alarming insight. He could see the poor boy's mind laid bare like a projected image in front of him. There were skyscrapers packed together, jostling against each other in some menacing, crowded and besieged cityscape. It made Frank feel claustrophobic just looking. They reached high, blotting out the sun, and worse, they had no windows, just terrible cracks and fissures that made everything seem unstable. Some of the cracks seemed familiar. Frank squinted and realised they were words. Hundreds of words on the side of the buildings that went on and on into the horizon and up and up into space. An oppresive confused epidemic of graffiti.

The poor boy must be going mad, having such a packed and unruly metropolis in his cranium. Perhaps he had spent too long looking at the absurd Tower of Light. Then he realised that they weren't skyscrapers at all; they were lists. The boy thought only in lists, as if life was a vast shopping expedition.

"My name's Trevor Bottom, Dr Finch," the poor creature said.

"And you are close to barking insanity, my dear boy. I,

Teresias, old man with wrinkled dugs, see all. Now sit down and I'll make some rosehip tea, then we'll discuss how to rid you of all these ridiculous lists. Would you care for a painkiller or two? I find them indispensable just recently."

Trevor's mouth opened and he gaped. This truly was his Dark Angel. He could read his mind. How could he possibly have known about the lists otherwise? Trevor almost wept with relief. He felt he could tell this mystical soul mate and mentor everything and he would be understood.

Chapter Nineteen

Saturday was warm and already Nora was regretting taking her mum out. It was hard work pushing the wheelchair across the bumpy common, but also the air seemed to invigorate her and make her even more cantankerous than she was at home.

"Is that a boy or a girl?" boomed her mother as they approached a young man with pink spiked hair, frayed denim and a little chain reaching from an impaled ear to an impaled nostril.

Nora closed her eyes and hoped Mum would shut up.

"And why has she got a lavatory chain pinned to her face? Is she some sort of mental patient?"

"I'm so sorry," whispered Nora as they passed the young man.

"Soroihgt, I know what they're loik without their medication," he said, and heaved a gobbet of mucus on the grass.

"What did she say?" demanded Mum.

"*He* said perhaps you should take up meditation," said Nora. Then she froze. Less than twenty yards away Brimley was walking towards them with his wife. She knew it was his wife because of the family photograph in his office. The first time they had made love there, he had turned it face down. Her first thought was to leave Mum and run. Then she thought perhaps she should just put her head down and keep walking. He might not even see her. God knows he wasn't the most observant of men. Even if he did, she could just smile a greeting and walk on. Two colleagues meeting accidentally. The only problem was the tight, breathless knot her heart had suddenly become. She couldn't bear it, the way his eyes would register then retreat from her. She veered off the path and into some bushes.

"What? What is it? Where are we going?" shouted her mother.

"Be quiet, Mum, please."

"Why should I, when you've just frightened the life out of me.

What are you going to do now? Leave me here? A poor old woman who sacrificed everything for her one and only daughter ..."

"Shut the fuck up!" Nora spat.

Her mum gaped and began weeping softly. Tears were much better. At least Nora could think. He'd said his wife was going away and clearly she hadn't. She never was, of course. She knew Brimley lied all the time, but it didn't matter usually. The lies were part of the understanding, just as she knew that he rarely thought about her except when she was there. She accepted that, and the fact that their affair would never go beyond the odd fumble and grope in the office, the very occasional coupling in a two star hotel. It was fine, she told herself. He liked her to mother him at work and it gave her a kind of pleasure to do so. Sometimes she imagined he was her child. It was easier then to be the Comforter, the Helpmate, the Listener. Like any conspiracy, it was shared.

Now, seeing him walking with his wife (there they went, him saying something about the book he was writing and how exhausting it all was for him), the concreteness of it, the sheer physical fact, was too real. He would go home with her, they would eat, talk to their children, go to bed together. It was a life, and she was so outside it. She scarcely existed for him. She had a sudden desire to be open, to just for once have everything laid bare.

She thought of coming out of the bushes, going straight up to them and saying, "Hello Brimley, how are your bowels, my love? And has that little festering mole on your left buttock healed yet?" But she knew she wouldn't. Couldn't. It wasn't in her.

There was another feeling, more disturbing. She realised she didn't like Brimley. His pinched spirit, the way he enjoyed exercising his little bit of power over others. At first she had been excited that a professor, albeit one of Quality Assurance, had wanted her, but the truth was he didn't really want *her*. She was just there. It was convenient.

She was angry. Perhaps she had always been angry and only now was allowing herself to acknowledge it, and a flurry of sensations and possibilities and new thoughts filled her. She was amazed at what was happening in her own mind.

Trevor spent the weekend in a fever of reading and thinking and feeling.

Frank had been exactly what he was looking for. He had told him that list making was an extremely useful and intellectually tidy way to organise thought but must not be an end in itself. Trev said he didn't think he could stop himself. Frank said it was a habit he had to contain and that, over the weekend, whenever he felt a compulsion to write a list, he should read a few more pages of Virgil's *Aeneid,* in order to see how Classical heroes overcame setbacks, and he should return on Monday morning for a progress report. It was wonderful to have someone offering practical advice which was also so interesting.

He read in translation of Aeneas's shipwreck on the north African coast, of his search for a new land in the west, of Dido falling hopelessly in love with him, of how strength came from bearing the test of woes, of how the gods were as capricious as people, sometimes more so. Frank said that a good mind could be both critically dispassionate and emotionally involved, so he made notes on style. But he also imagined himself on the sail-fledged sea searching for his promised land in the welcoming arms and, hopefully, thighs of Cynth. It was all so much better than being humiliated by pimps and security guards. Perhaps I'll become an academic, he thought.

Frank was on his knees and appeared to be listening to the heating pipes when Trev arrived on Monday. Trev coughed and Frank looked up at him, startled. He seemed pale, as if he hadn't slept much, and his eyes were large and glassy.

"Trevor Bottom, Dr Finch. I came to see you. You told me to read the *Aeneid.*"

"Very wise of me," said Frank.

He seemed to see something in Trev's mind, something large. It moved. It was a woman.

"Ah. You're in love, dear boy," said Frank.

"How did you know?" asked Trev, gaping.

"It doesn't matter, and speak low, if you speak of love."

"Why?"

"Because Shakespeare tells us to. It's an act of reverence. Of course love is also saucy and bawdy."

"How do you know when it's which?"

"You have to read the moods of love," said Frank. "Is it reciprocal?"

"Sort of. I mean – at some deep level I think she's mad about me, it's just she doesn't know it yet."

"I see. Then you must be constant, *con amore*, until she gives you a sign. Euripides tells us that he is not a lover who does not love forever." A picture of Margaret came to him. She was throwing a ball for Jemma, their little Spaniel (now sadly gone too), and suddenly she turned to smile at him. You can be in love with the dead too, he realised. Praising what is lost makes the remembrance dear.

"How do you think I can sort of get her to notice me?" asked Trev.

"It's obvious, my dear boy. You must first notice yourself. Celebrate yourself. Nietzsche tells us that love is the creative force that keeps life itself alive. The will to love can help you see the lovable side of life; otherwise you will only see what is ugly and repulsive."

"Nietzsche? But I thought he was a Nazi."

"The ignorant are everywhere," said Frank. "That's why you should read." He looked at his bookshelves. "Art helps you to live. Even disenchantments can have a metaphysical magic. Art is a bridge back to the self and prevents succumbing to nihilist ennui. What's the time?"

"Nearly ten," said Trev.

Frank paled. He seemed to shrink.

"You must go now. The underworld waits. I need to prepare."

He took a painkiller from his pocket and swallowed it.

Trev left, both cheered and baffled. Dr Finch was obviously a nutter, prone to scary mood swings, but Trev liked him, and amongst the nuttiness there was something worth listening to.

A knock on Frank's door. It was ten o'clock. This is what he had been dreading. He looked around at his books, hoping they might leap off the shelves to defend him. He took another painkiller, his fourth already this morning.

Before he could swallow it properly the door was pushed open and in walked General Vittorio Spinelli, followed by two men so large you could not encompass either one of them with a single look. Your eyes had to pan across and up and down to appreciate the sheer scale. They entered, ducking to get in the door, and flanked the General, looming above him. Frank gazed from one to the other. They were twins so identical it beggared belief, or buggered it completely, as Frank thought. Massive bodies in black suits, large square closely cropped heads, dark unmoving eyes. The one on the General's right had a scar that went all across his face and continued across his brother's. Someone had obviously taken an almighty slash with a cutlass or sword when they had been standing close together. Frank dared not think what they did in return.

These were the General's bodyguards, Boris and Boris Venyvich, Bulgarian escapees from the new liberal regime, both wanted for crimes against humanity.

The General himself had an oily smile, a dark yellowish complexion, thin black moustache, and dangerous dancing eyes. He wore crisply ironed cavalry twill trousers, a striped Roebuck University tie, and an oversized blazer with the Roebuck crest – or Adam's logo as it was now called – on the pocket, depicting the Tower of Light. His black patent shoes shone like scrubbed coals. His little ratty eyes danced from side to side and took in everything.

So far he had been disappointed in the university. He had imagined oak panelled libraries hosting great and solemn thoughts, narrow cobbled paths beneath rose-entwined arches, themselves shadowed by Gothic spires and illuminated by stained glass, scholars in ermine-collared gowns and genuflecting students in black robes flocking like eager starlings to feast on intellectual riches. What he found was bland modernity and shuffling crowds of denim and sportswear adorning bodies that knew nothing of sport. It was all very disappointing.

At least Dr Finch looked intelligent, perhaps even wise. Most of all, Spinelli coveted wisdom. He was tired of opening European newspapers and seeing cartoons of himself as the dwarf tyrant. He could have sent emissaries to garrotte those responsible, for the world was small these days and everything was possible, but paradoxically he wanted their love and admiration. He thought that if he returned home with a PhD from an English university, things would be different. At home people would obey him because they thought him wise, and not because he could have their most intimate body parts crushed to a pulp. Abroad the view of him would slowly metamorphose too. In his secret dreams he even thought the Nobel Peace Prize might be within his grasp after a few years of benign rule and cash handouts to the right people.

Studying Virgil had first suggested itself through his horse, also called Virgil. The General had loved that horse more than he'd ever loved a human being, and he still mourned him and carried his ashes in a little silver pot wherever he went. Secondly, he'd overheard two diplomats talking and one said Virgil was the epitome of civilised heroism. The phrase appealed to his vanity and his imagination.

These were the General's secret thoughts, which his idiosyncratic grasp of English had not yet allowed him to communicate to anyone in England. He wanted to leave the General behind and emerge, butterflylike, as the Wise Prophet. The General kept asserting himself, however, and old habits were proving hard to eradicate.

He bowed elaborately.

"Doctorr Feench. Iss my great 'onour to meeting this one eminenté expert on Virgil and his Aeneid. I feel 'onour in the presence of – 'ow you should say – intellectual giant. Eet make me feel I should cut off my testicles in your presence, though I musta say I expect you 'ave grander office with many wimmins at word processorings to record your thoughts. Still, ees the Engleesh way, no, to be 'umble? 'Ow you say – self defecating.

"Thees two mens are my personal assistants at all times they are with me but weel make no noise unless I tell thems. Ees Boris and annuder Boris Venyvich. Professor Trevalyans 'e say you get my docto*rrr*ate on the roads pretty double quick times. 'Ow we should begin?"

Frank was caught. Trapped. This greasy, unspeakable mass murderer was actually here, present. It was definitely happening. He wondered if by merely breathing the same air he would become a killer and torturer himself. He imagined the General laughing over a mass of steaming offal he had just removed from a political opponent. Completely irrational questions coursed through his mind. He wanted to ask, "How many people have you killed personally?" "Is it true that you have a small penis and that's why men like you behave so abominably? Is it really that absurdly, banally, grotesquely simple?" "Why on earth do you want a PhD from an English university?" "Are you going to beat people to death with your parchment degree scroll or strangle them with your robe?"

But he did none of this. He suggested the General prepare a translation of part of Book Five of the Aeneid, where Aeneas presses on to Italy after Juno has made the women of Sicily set fire to many of his ships. He wondered what gods the man worshipped. They agreed that the General would return in two days time. He left, but Frank was sure the smell of death stayed in his office.

Chapter Twenty

At first he didn't know what the laughter was about. As he walked through the Student Union club, he had been imagining Cynth as Lavinia, tending the altar-fire, her royal locks all alight, her coronal, with jewels bright, and him coming across the oceans of the world for her. He would woo and win her quickly, in the manner of a hero, and their nuptials would be great cause for feasting and drinking among the crew, and his warriors would sing old songs of love and war and death as he and Cynth went below for a first night of exquisite rapture. Vigorous sexual intercourse on a high sea would be a fine thing. One of the great benefits of literature, he thought, is that it can enrich your own fantasy life.

What the hell were they laughing at?

When he first turned and saw it on the big screen, it took a good five seconds for his brain to unscramble the image, take the familiar figures and put them in this new cinematic context. The point of view was from above but the image was clear. Cynth was pushed up against the side of a lift and Damien was jammed against her, rubbing himself up and down slightly. His right hand was massaging her left breast and he was kissing her fiercely. Trev concentrated on the details to avoid taking in the full measure of the digital tape: the stray lock of hair on her forehead; the pink folder she grasped in her left hand; her white trainers.

A cheer went up from the watching students, then a boo of disappointment as the tape finished, then a small cheer as it looped back and began again. Trev sat and watched it through three times before the thoughts and questions started to form like little crystals in his brain.

How long had it been going on? How could he not have known? He had watched his beloved like a shark circling its prey – he'd never seen Damien go to her room, nor she to his. There had been no signs of passion exchanged between them during seminars. Did they only do it in lifts? How often had they done it – actually done it?

As his dreams turned to ashes, he felt a physical desire to make lists. Long, long lists that went on for centuries and could cross continents, lists that would sort, arrange and quantify the myriad levels of his anguish, lists that dripped blood with an intensity of heartbreak, lists of darkness. He would be a collector of pain, a cataloguer of misery. He needed to see his Dark Angel.

Jeremy Pickles watched the tape of Cynth and Damien on his CCTV monitor and decided to do nothing. It didn't amount to much. It was all relative. God, what some of these students got up to in toilets and wheelie bins and car parks would make a hooker wince. This was peanuts.

He knew that one or more of the security guards had decided to spool it into the internal university television network as a joke. He could discover exactly who it was and sack them, but security guards were a strange breed. There seemed to be many more of them than he had actually employed, and he was sure some of them carried weapons. Things were going so well lately that it seemed politic to leave well alone for now.

Once the master plan was in operation, the Final Solution, then he would just cream off the most reliable guards as a sort of personal army. For now, let it be. Just the Creative Writing tutor groping someone fat in a lift. Nevertheless he felt unsettled. The odd thing about power was that, while you encircled yourself with it as protection, it could also be a threatening ring of flame.

In the Tower of Light, Adam Bittermouth looked at Damien rubbing against Cynth and quickly flicked to a university PR channel showing happy students smiling and pointing up at the Tower. He knew the image of the groping in the lift would stay with him, like a high speed tumour it would grow for several hours and he would fear the roof was lowering, that the Dark Invader was sharpening his instruments of death up there, but then it would burst and the two people in the lift would be just another confirmation that messy intimacy, gravity and death were all outside, and he would be safe again.

Damien opened his post and there were the fat thing's poems, and a note from Frank: *Dear Boy, these are excellent. The raw, explosive talent of a mind that has a long way to travel, but the getting there will be an exciting odyssey for all readers.* Damien smirked. If that fat wallop could write poetry worth reading, he'd do something outrageous, like give a month's salary – such as it was, the bastards – to charity.

He started to read and, exactly one hour later, took out his chequebook and wrote one for two pounds to the Devon Donkey Sanctuary. After all, he reasoned to himself, he was only speaking figuratively, as a poet should, when he said a month's salary. Two quid would feed a donkey for a few days at least. I mean, what do they eat? Just grass and hay and crap anyway. Two quid was generous. More to the point, the poems were really very good. How could a bovine lump write stuff like this?

He started to feel resentful. It really wasn't fair to put such talent in a ridiculous body like that. For Christ's sake, what could she possibly have ever done that was vaguely interesting, except been kissed by him? That was probably the climax of her life so far, whereas he had already experienced verdant pastures, strange worlds, mad dreams, numerous nubile young bodies. He was a poet warrior. He had the attitude, the *je ne sais quoi*, the looks, the *right* to talent. Well, she could wait for her poems.

In fact … yes, why not? He reached for a large brown envelope.

Chapter Twenty-One

It was going very badly. Brimley had gone to interview eminent children's writer Ronald Drain in order to gather materials crucial to his biography. It was six months overdue and the publishers were making noises.

He had found the old man in his worst mood yet. Drain went down to his shed and refused to see Brimley at first until Mrs Drain – the third, and most patient yet – coaxed him out with strong tea and a plate of cupcakes. He now sat scowling, his eyes like nuggets of chocolate in a chip cookie, and Brimley had to constantly check his natural inclination to be rude, which in turn made him feel highly stressed. Also, it was now six days since any sniff of a bowel movement and everything felt leaden. It was starting to get to the familiar stage of miserable desperation.

"Can you tell me something about characterisation?" Brimley asked.

"Absolutely not!" said Drain, spitting crumbs.

"How do you get your characters?"

"'Get?' How do I 'get' them? As if it's like going to the fucking supermarket and 'getting' something, like soap powder or cheese biscuits. What the sodding bastard hell do you mean – 'get'?"

Drain scowled at Brimley contemptuously.

"Are they based on people you know? *The Giant Who Hated Children*, for example. Is that based on someone?" He just managed to avoid saying *yourself.*

"You mean is it me?" said Drain, sharp as ninepence. "Of course it is, you cretin, and if you say so I'll sue the scraggy arse off you."

God, it was so wearying. Why had he thought it would be a doddle to write a literary biography of this old cunt?

"Can you tell me about your audience? Do you have a specific child in mind when you write?"

"Child? What are you talking about? Haven't you been listening? Can't stand children. Hate the little bastards. I write what I know will sell."

Brimley took out a copy of Drain's book, *Chunky and the Cheese Factory*.

"What was the inspiration for this – probably your best seller to date?"

Drain looked at the book as if it was a turd. He took it and turned it over.

"Did I write this?" he said, genuinely perplexed.

Brimley pointed to the name on the cover.

"Ha!" exploded Drain, and another mouthful of cupcake sprayed Brimley. "I'll be buggered. Doesn't ring a bell at all. What's it about?"

"It's about … never mind," said Brimley, feeling suddenly old and weary. He wished Nora would walk in with her sweet, long suffering smile and a large mug of coffee.

Drain was eyeing him like something moving in for the kill.

"I'll tell you how I 'get' characters. I visualise people as animals. You, for example, look like a constipated ferret."

"Why did you say constipated?" asked Brimley, wondering if his affliction was visible.

"Because you look all stuck in and jammed up and pinched. I bet the last time your wife got a good rodgering was the day before she met you," said Drain.

"Now, this sickly ferret, this constipated, ineffectual runt, is the only creature on the river bank with absolutely no talent at all. The others can either run, or hunt, or build, or even write books, like the clever old fox Ronaldo, but this runt can't do a thing for itself, so it just lives off the others. Feeds on their scraps, lives off them, like a maggot, like a parasite, like a runt. And do you know what I'm going to call this cunt of a runt?

"I think I'd better go," said Brimley.

"Not yet you won't. I'm just getting warmed up. There's

money to be made here," said Drain, and crammed another cupcake in his mouth.

Cynth wondered what the hell was going on. She had gone to the campus supermarket to replenish the contents of the sacred and terrible tin, the dark call of Ely Cathedral. She had a carrier bag with a Mint Crunchie, three Double Deckers, two Flakes, a Picnic, three fudge bars and a packet of Chocolate Buttons, and was hugging it guiltily as she walked across the Student Union bar. A few girls giggled at her, then a red-faced lad with mad ginger hair pointed her out to his mates and they started whispering to each other. People stopped what they were doing and looked.

Somewhere a drink was spilled. Eyes were everywhere. Then Helen, the girl from the Creative Writing group, fell into step with her and started chatting.

"Hiya," she said.

Cynth gave her a quick look and walked on.

"Not much of a chatterbox, are you? Still, some of us can't stop, like. Me ma says I came out, like, talking for England. Me and me mates are going to see Withering Dong tonight in the Falklands Bar. Fancy coming? They're a reet good band."

Cynth blushed and shook her head. Was this a wind up? What was going on? Helen didn't seem at all put off by the refusal.

"Fair enough," said Helen. "Prob'ly got better things on, eh? Reet dark horse you are. See y'around."

She peeled away and Cynth went down to the lake and sat eating a Cadbury Flake, watching the Canada geese stir from the water and waddle like a marooned armada to another stretch, honking their territorial claims. Something had happened. Something had changed. Her place in the world had shifted and she could find no explanation for it. It was strange to be alive. She looked up and could see Dad walking towards her, smiling in that confident, but slightly shy way, and if he had sat down next to her, maybe took her arm, she could ask: "What is it that makes people real?"

High above her, from the panoramic window view of

Bittermouth Universal House, Roebuck's showcase apartments for corporate clients, or the odd fantastically wealthy student (five-star accommodation, multi-choice menu, view of the lake, great earner), General Spinelli looked down and saw her.

"Boris, bring me a camera," he said.

Chapter Twenty-Two

Frank thought of trying to pretend he was out, or sick, or dead. Anything to stop the unspeakable General Spinelli coming for another tutorial with his thuggish bodyguards, his swaggering brutalising of the beloved *Aeneid*, the stink of his cigarillos. But it was no good, and he now sat miserably listening to the little tyrant. Boris and Boris flanked the door and stared noncommittally at Frank as the General paced up and down, oleaginous skin glistening, translation in his hand, proclaiming as if auditioning for an over-acting award.

"A womans is like a tree Aeneas mounts 'igh.

'Is semens go 'omeward up her leafy thighs …

Iss good, yes, Doctorr Feench?"

"It's an interesting, one might say radical, translation," said Frank.

Spinelli beamed at his henchmen.

"See boys, I iss one – 'ow you say – innoventive transerlator. Radical, you 'ear that? But not communisto, eh, Doctorr? Ha ha ha!"

Frank tried to introduce a note of intellectual enterprise, as opposed to off the wall sexual fantasy, into the translation.

"'*Hic viridem Aeneas frondenti ex ilice metam, Constituit signum nautis pater; unde reverti Scirent, et longos ubi circumflectere cursu*s.' To translate: 'Good Aeneas sets a bough of ilex upon the steep, green leaved and tall, which is a goal, or sign, for the sailors to steer by.' It is nothing to do with mounting and semen," said Frank with a stiff smile.

"Si, si, Doctorr, just a detail different 'ere and there. 'Ow you say – a truffle?"

"Trifle," said Frank. "If you could continue …"

"Si. Hokay. Lessee now. *Nudatosque humeros … Considunt*

transstris …The captains 'e is one 'omosexual boy and 'e get excited when 'e put the wet oil on his naked sailors and probe them whores good, all pantings and the big throbbings," declaimed Spinelli, his smile suddenly fading. "'Ey, Doctorr, 'ow come thees captains is one queer 'omosexual? 'E meant to be big 'ero and not the bottoms boy. In my country we chop 'is privates and cook them for the dogs. I mean in the old days."

"He is not a homosexual," said Frank, losing the will to live. "A more apt translation might be "The captains, gaily decked in purple and gold. The crews their brows with poplar garlands twine …""

"Si, si. Hokay," interrupted Spinelli. "But this very boring. When we go to 'ell, Doctorr Feench? To the inferno?"

"Beg pardon?" asked Frank, fearing the worst.

"I ham pantings at the leash to go to 'ell. I 'ave the big itchings for it. Book Six. When Aeneas go to 'ell and see what them devils do to the sons of bitches who cross the 'ero. I ham wantings to do the big transerlation of this and see what this devils do to them bastards."

Frank had a sudden insight into what the General really wanted: a greater sense of hell than he already had and an array of new tortures. That and to indulge the mistaken notion that Virgil wrote mainly about peculiar sex. It was all too much. It was such a travesty of everything Frank knew and loved.

It was as if the General intuited his thoughts. He looked at Frank and smiled greasily.

"We iss mens of the world. We know issa 'ard. But iff we iss understandings all thees killings and wotnottings then we become wise. Yess? We understandings what 'uman beans iss. Like gods we iss all knowings – 'ow you say – him-potent."

This hopelessly muddled deification of his own psychotic urges did nothing to console Frank, and when Trev arrived an hour later he was on his knees. Before Trev could speak, Frank shushed him and listened to the heating pipes. He seemed to be conducting an imaginary orchestra.

"Dr Finch, I'm here because I'm desperate," said Trev after a few minutes.

"It is the human condition, dear boy. Now listen. You hear? Da da da da. Just that soft mournful pulse. Mozart. *The Requiem*. It is the music of Death. The beat of mortality. Listen. That doom laden melodic climb, like Death's weary footsteps. It is all around us."

Trev got on his knees and listened. He heard a lot of gurgling and sploshing and burping, as if a tribe of noisy dwarves were in a state of flatulent abandon. But then he listened more closely and could hear something. Not music, but voices, far off, distant, a babble. Very odd. He looked up but Frank had gone to his desk and was swallowing pills from a brown bottle.

"Are you feeling all right, Dr Finch?"

"Inasmuch as I feel violated and that everything I hold dear has been spat upon and scorned by a spineless hypocrisy astonishing only in its lack of guilt; in that every principle about education, indeed, about life itself that I have tried to steer by has, in this very room, recently been put to the sword by the forces of iniquity; in that my little shrine to knowledge has been infected by a psychotic elf and his ugly chuffing twins from hell, then *yes*, I feel fine, my boy. In the pink. But I see from your clammy demeanour that all does not bode well in affairs of the heart."

"I can't believe it. She's been … she's been at it. With someone else. I don't know what to do," said Trev pitifully.

"Cervantes tells us that love and war are the same thing, and stratagems and policy are as allowable in one as in the other," said Frank.

"So I should have a plan, as if I'm in a war?" Trev was clutching at straws.

Frank looked down at the liver spots on the backs of his hands. How many times they had held Margaret, David their son, brushed away their tears, held great books, lifted the blue china teapot for two? He might be a coward but his hands had not betrayed anyone, even though the left one trembled a little. I'm just doing my job, he thought, but how many times through the ages had that been said? And in the quiet of the dark night he knew that supervising Spinelli was an unholy betrayal. Trev coughed and Frank looked up.

"A plan? Certainly. You can either wallow in despair and self pity or you can do something."

"Like what?"

"Thought is action, and time spent in its pursuit will suggest what physical actions, if any, should follow. You have a rival, my boy, and you must assess your own strengths and weaknesses, and your adversary's, and then pit your strengths against his weaknesses.

"From Virgil we see that the hero must use his own brains and muscles when the gods can do no more. Like Aeneas, do not slash at shadows, but keep your mind on your enemy. And then, unleash *duo fulmina belli*, the twin thunderbolts of battle. Justice, revenge, following your heart, one can read the Classics as superb literary texts and as rollicking adventures. Perhaps they are telling you to act. Here – a gift."

He gave Trev a little leather bound copy of *The Aeneid*.

It was a lovely present, but Dr Finch was off his chump. Trev knew that, looking at the flakes of dandruff on his jacket collar, the little stain on his shirt. But there was something about the old man – a frail but noble spirit, a crumbling but interesting mind. He was about something. He seemed to believe in things, albeit in a demented sort of way. Also, perhaps most significantly, he seemed to care about Trev's plight and give him a sense of mission.

It wasn't all over with Cynth necessarily. He was at war. After all, hadn't Dr Finch said the words *war, battle, revenge*? Trev would pursue all of these, he decided. Then, when the battle had been bloodily won, there would be tearful remonstrations and wrenching confessions with Cynth, but these would end in sex even more passionate because of the emotional intensity that heartache engendered. And then, in some peaceful future, the Yorkshire terriers snoring at his feet, he would dig deep into himself and write about it all. He would give it all back to the world.

Chapter Twenty-Three

Roy Fish had a nose for things. Secrets, rumours, information, injustices. He could sniff them out; nudge them from corners of corners that no one else even saw.

A high forehead that ski sloped down to the tip of his nose in one curved line gave him the sleek appearance of a shark on the prowl. He seemed to move without walking, to glide and suddenly appear beside people, making them feel guilty, perhaps for some long ago incident or word or thought, and with an uncanny sense that Fish knew all about it and now was the moment of reckoning. He even unnerved Jeremy Pickles. His antennae were out now, his radar finely tuned, his snout feeling the thermals as he moved softly past the dribbling plastic fountain, through the fluorescent lit plastic tables, the Formica salads and glutinous pies of the Bittermouth Eatery.

He had been sitting next to him for more than a minute before Frank realised Roy Fish was there, and he almost jumped from his seat. Frank's left hand, clutching a white plastic fork above an anaemic tomato and something limp that wanted to be pasta, started to tremble slightly, a fact which Fish could not fail to notice.

"Frank, melancholic Frank, is this the mask of grief or have the powers that be given you some odious task that will rot your brains faster than whatever it is you are imbibing?" asked Fish knowingly.

Frank looked at him, startled. He was just getting used to knowing what was in people's minds himself; it was disconcerting that Fish could do it too, but through intelligent deduction rather than pharmaceutically induced phantasmagoria.

"Dilated pupils, Frank, speak volumes. Tell me. I'm here."

"It's nothing," lied Frank.

He tried to form an impression of Fish's mind but it was too layered, too dense, too protected – a Berlin wall with powerful searchlights scanning the world.

"My question to you is this: Is Trevalyan the bullying lymphoma we all suspected he would be?" Fish asked.

"Yes, quite. Unpleasant enough, but just doing his job, I suppose."

"But not *coram populo*, Frank, eh? Furtively, like a spider."

"That's right," said Frank.

"And what has he got you to do, in particular?"

"Nothing, in particular," said Frank defensively, trying to avoid the slanted white lamps of Fish's predatory look. The man had a way of getting things out of you. It was disconcerting, although Frank always thought that, despite the hard edges, Fish was on the side of the angels. At least he was clever.

"Any new courses you have to teach?" asked Fish.

"No."

"Pressure to publish?"

"Not really."

"New postgrads?"

Frank winced. His left hand trembled a little more.

"Not to speak of."

"I touch a nerve. Corduroy trousers, a last fine book from a good mind, a cellar of Chablis and Crozes Hermitage, apple trees and forsythia," said Fish.

"What?" asked Frank, knowing perfectly well.

"Your last year or so here. It's how I envisaged it, how we both did, how it should be. The lessening of responsibilities before the dignified stroll to retirement, but then the state of Denmark rotted and Eden became Hades. What is the last word in the Oxford Popular?"

"Zygote," said Frank. "A cell formed by the union of two gametes."

"And the last word in the Collins English Gem, pocket edition, first published 1902?"

"I'm not sure," said Frank. "Zulu?"

"Zymotic. Zymotic, Frank. Think about it. Fermenting disease created by the multiplication of germs introduced from without. From the Greek Zumotikos. My question to you is this: why would they start to expunge this ancient word from our lexicon? It was in the Pocket Gem, but not in the later, vastly bigger Oxford Popular. Why? Think about it."

"The lexicographer considered it to be archaic?" suggested Frank.

Fish snorted derisively, throwing back his long smooth head, like a lazy anaconda letting something large and still undead slide slowly down his gullet.

"It's a scientific term. It's relevant, Frank, pertinent. That's why they are trying to eradicate it. Disease introduced from without. It is precisely what is happening here, under the gobbledygook of rationalising knowledge and enquiry into kowtowing number crunching. They are taking away our word for it – zymotic. An ancient word that still has the ghost of old civilizations, the weight of history, the pursuit of knowledge, the cradle of high culture … and it tells us what they are doing. Infecting us from the top down. Zymotic. It's happening in government, industry, and now here, in what some still laughingly call a seat of learning."

"I'm not really a conspiracy theorist, Roy."

"Of course you are, Frank."

"But you seriously think that the Chancellor and the Registrar are consciously part of some huge network that involves the civil service, the government, publishers, Uncle Tom Cobbley and all, to neutralise our language so we don't realise how we are being diminished, deprived of our intelligence and ultimately, our humanity?"

"Take out the word 'consciously', Frank old boy, and you've got it in one. They don't know they're doing it. They're not clever enough for that. That's why it's so insidious. They aren't even aware of their own primitive unconscious impulses. We are being driven to ruin by amoebae with laptops. You know it's true, Frank. English is a non-subject, a girl's subject, a degree for people who don't know what to do, the domestic science of academe. But I've always known you to be a clever man; you are a beacon in a stew of dead fish. Think about it. Now what about this new student? What's his name?"

"Spin…" Frank almost said the terrible word – Spinelli – but stopped himself in time. Fish had almost tricked him.

"Spin-what, Frank? Spin doctor? Spin bowler? Spinster? A foreign name, is it?"

Frank looked down at his trembling left hand and felt sorry for it in a detached way. Poor trembling creature. What was the point? Fish would find out, and why am I being so secretive about it, anyway?

"Spinelli," said Frank, looking around in case spies had their digital recorders trained on him.

Even Roy Fish was impressed.

"Not General (Murdering Bastard Fascist Killing Fields Torturing CIA-backed Raping Arsehole of the World) Spinelli?"

"One and the same. I believe they are holding the announcement back a little, waiting for a bad news day. They probably won't use his real name either. He's doing a PhD on the *Aeneid*. I'm his supervisor. He is a cretin. It is sending me barking mad. O! Let me not be mad, not mad, sweet heaven. At least I have the solace of the pipes," said Frank, almost to himself.

"Pipes?" asked Fish.

"You'll hear them too. When you're ready."

Fish decided to ignore this tangential thought.

"The question I put to you is this: Why? What do they get out of Spinelli being here?"

"I don't know," said Frank. "Certainly not kudos."

"And not power. Which leaves money," said Fish.

"You think he's paying more than the ordinary fees?" asked Frank. "Isn't that illegal?"

"Legality is simply the place where the goalposts are moved. I bet he's giving them a small fortune. They'll hide it, of course, in some ridiculous fund or other. Once you go public on this, Frank, we'll know more."

"Public! I want to keep it a secret. I want it to go away."

"You have no choice," said Fish. "It's an outrage. We will create a stink that will flush out all the toadying apparatchiks involved. It's an opportunity, Frank."

"No. I just want to get through it as quietly and as painlessly as possible. I'm sorry, but there it is. I have to get back now. I think I hear the beginning of Vaughan Williams' *Lark Ascending* and they won't wait forever."

"Who won't?"

"The pipes, of course."

Frank left, still clutching his plastic fork.

In his office Jeremy Pickles watched Frank walk away on the CCTV screen and looked carefully at Roy Fish, trying to discern what might have been said. It was ridiculous that they couldn't get sound too. Fish had that rapacious, predatory air about him. He knew something. Frank must have talked. He'd regret it. But how much had he said?

Chapter Twenty-Four

Nora took in a mug of extra strong Columbian, a little bowl of dried apricots and prunes and two glycerine suppositories folded discreetly in a napkin. Brimley was at his desk miserably trying to write his great book about the despicable Drain, but all he could see when he tried to think were gloriously flushing toilet cisterns.

"Nothing?" asked Nora.

"No, and the book is as stuck as I am," said Brimley, realising how much he had come to value Nora's self-sacrificing, undemanding, unselfish solicitude (all those beautiful negatives in one woman). Made him feel something approaching tenderness. She seemed almost real to him in a way he had never countenanced before. He wondered what sort of person she might be if one were to really get to know her.

"And how was the weekend?" she asked, and thought: *Please don't lie. Please don't lie. Please don't lie. If you just tell me the truth things can carry on. This will be enough. I will be satisfied. Just think enough of me to tell me. Please.*

"Horrendous," said Brimley. "Helen away all the bloody time, the kids a nightmare. I'm exhausted, Nora. And to think *we* could have had a night together but …" He made an expansive gesture with his hand.

She smiled as she always smiled. *The moment is gone.*

"It's a week since I've had a movement," said Brimley, wanting to enjoy Nora's sympathy a little longer.

"You poor thing. Perhaps you should consider the colonic again."

"I told you, I'm not having a strange woman shoving a hosepipe up my anus and then having to pay for the privilege."

"It needn't be like that. I know her very well. I could borrow the equipment and do it myself, here, in your office. We could lock the door and no one need ever know."

"But you've never done it before."

"It's really not that complicated. I'd get Shamina to give me precise instructions. But if you don't want to ..." Nora began tidying papers.

"I didn't say that. I was just expressing reservations. It does seem to be getting worse. I'm sick of pain and discomfort. How much will it cost?"

"Nothing. Not if it's me. I'll do it for love."

"You're such a ... good thing," said Brimley awkwardly. "Let's say tomorrow evening. About six thirty. No one will be around then."

Tomorrow was Tuesday, Nora's reading group evening, but she could miss it for once. *Great Expectations* could wait.

Chapter Twenty-Five

Jeremy Pickles liked meetings. They gave him an almost religious sense of order. Being a Buddhist must feel like this, he thought, when he entered the room and sat at the head of the big oval table. Or even better, the Pope.

He was especially pleased because this was the first formal CRAP meeting, meaning the master plan, the Final Solution, was beginning to take material shape. From idea to execution. Such a satisfying arc. Everything in its place: the Roebuck paper pad and new, sharp Roebuck pencil before each chair; the small bottle of Bittermouth Evian with its Icarus logo and napkin; the bowl of dried fruit (he must stop Brimley Trevalyan scoffing the lot as he usually tried to do); chairs pleasingly equidistant apart and from the table. A specially prepared big screen with digital remote so that Jeremy could zap up diagrams, flow charts and data. Sometimes he would deliberately include a completely nonsensical graph but predictably no one noticed, and a few would even nod sagely at the gobbledygook. That was fun.

He sat on his hands and tried to suck in his cheeks, allowed a murmur of conversation, then cleared his throat and stood up. It was a carefully chosen group. Brimley from English, a useful hatchet man, then mostly harmless yes-people from various places, who would listen dutifully, make fatuous points just to reassure themselves they had made a "contribution", and then Jeremy and the Chancellor could do what the hell they liked with the Spinelli money in pursuit of the Final Solution.

He looked around. Apart from he and Brimley, there was Vincent Grub from Geography (wimp), Helma Snotwinger from Biology (cretin), Chris Thodd from Drama and the Performing Arts (complete tosser), Julia Narnett from Law (ambitious – would gladly kill to get a Chair), Graham Perkes from Chemistry (nerd), and finally, Emily Wastehope from ... something was wrong. That was definitely not the bland and shapeless Emily Wastehope. That was, oh God, where was Emily Wastehope? This was Mercedes Blonk, the hideous meddling feminist with the droopy tits who never shuts up. No wonder the Ancients preferred boys, if there were women like Blonk about.

"I was expecting Emily Wastehope," said Pickles with a puzzled smile.

"And you've got me," said Mercedes. "As a senior member of staff, I do have the right to attend any meeting of a new committee."

Pickles looked icily at Brimley, who gave the faintest of shrugs and shifted uncomfortably in his seat.

"Of course you do," said Pickles. "I would have thought you had more important things to attend to, though: A celebrity quiz show – Big Sister or something."

"I'm curious. My intellect has a libido too, and it is well and truly aroused. I want to know about CRAP. I sense something happening here and my instincts are never wrong."

"You're quite right, CRAP is a bit of a groundbreaking move," said Pickles. "No point in pretending otherwise."

Mercedes smiled. Brimley looked quizzically at Pickles. Surely he wasn't just going to hand over the master plan without a fight?

"CRAP. Centre for Research in Academic Practice. What we wish to achieve, Doctor Blonk, is no less than a full initiation of sixteen, yes, no less than sixteen, working parties to explore the processes of embedding innovation in Roebuck. I shall detail each in turn. As you can see ..." He zapped up a meaningless graph full of lines, squiggles and figures that looked like a congealing bowl of spaghetti bolognaise.

"... First will be the sub-working party concerned with transferability, i.e. seeking alternative practices which allow for the redistribution of learning strategies over an inter-departmental affiliated structure of learning and resource management which will enhance, improve and quantify our commitment to service provision. You could chair that sub-working party, if you wish, Dr

Blonk. Or you might find the Alliance and Distance Learning Distribution Pack Committee more to your taste. I'll be detailing that in about, oh (*a glance at his digital watch that glows in the dark and has a voice activated recorder*), two and a half hours' time.

"In the meantime let's examine how the Committee for ICT or Inter-Corporate Transference, will help rationalise IT and CS in the proposed newly variegated HE proposals in the paper I distributed last term entitled *The Re-Organization of Multi-Purpose Quantifying Practices in Educational Transferability Management*. You have all read that paper?"

All nodded, except Mercedes. She yawned and Pickles smiled inwardly.

"Excellent. Then you'll be aware (*and here zapping up a flow chart that looked like a stupefied colon and made Brimley wince*) of Roebuck's intentions to diversify its commitment to the four sections of critical reflection outlined in the earlier paper, number RC351. Let's examine it point by point ..."

"Are you going to talk this crapspeak all afternoon?" asked Mercedes.

"CRAP is the language of education, Dr Blonk. Actually, it will probably go on into the early evening. We've a lot of ground to cover and I know none of you want to miss anything."

Murmurs of approval showed he was right.

"Then good luck to you," said Mercedes, rising and jangling like a plumber's tool belt as she left the room.

Pickles looked at those remaining. Now they could start. Never underestimate the power of boredom.

Damien was ecstatic. He did a little victory dance around his office. Penguin was going to publish him. Fucking Penguin Books! And they were going straight to paperback; so confident were they that the collection would find an audience. He looked at the letter again. Letters of gold, words of triumph: "Tough, muscular voice ... powerful, original images ... cadences that delight ..."

Ha ha! He was a made man. Even in the dark nights of his soul, he had anticipated this moment. He wanted to open the window and shout his triumph. He wanted champagne. He wanted a blowjob from Naomi Campbell. He wanted a Harley Davidson diamond studded World Cup photographic memory of this moment when the dream of dreams arrived. How could such joy be wrong? How could such a moment be compromised? It would be sacrilege.

There was the small problem of the hill of flesh. Suppose she kicked up a stink and said they were her poems? It was almost profane to spoil this pinnacle-of-life mood of victory, but he had to consider it. He would deny it. She was a nonentity, a literary stalker trying to plagiarise his great work. And in a crucial fundamental sense it *was* his work, even though he hadn't actually written it. He was Director of Creative Writing, so it stood to reason that any work produced during his course was, in a metaphysical and practical way, *his* work. He was the North Star, the shaman of their thoughts; without him they could do nothing. He was the facilitator, the sensibility at the centre of their writing. It was his work all right. Let any bastard try and say otherwise.

He put the publisher's letter in the pink folder of poems and slid it into his desk drawer. The world had beckoned and he would not disappoint. He decided to send an e-mail to Helen and ask her in tomorrow evening. With his confidence soaring like an eagle, he had no doubt he'd be rutting her senseless within half an hour of arrival. The evening after he'd ask in that post grad, Heidi, with the big tits. It was a grand week for the double.

Chapter Twenty-Six

Frank opened his internal mail. A memo from Roy Fish – one of the few people in the university who wrote letters rather than e-mail, and insisted on writing by hand, in copperplate pen and ink.

My Dear Frank,

A pleasure to see you yesterday, although my concern for your health and well being is compromised by the knowledge that you have to endure the presence of the pond scum Spinelli. God does not come out at all well in the Book of Job, and neither will we if we let this devil's spawn remain at Roebuck.

That our dear Registrar allowed Spinelli in confirms the suspicions of many that his brains, as well as his name, are pickled. The most illuminating conversation I have ever had with him about the university consisted of silence. We cannot appeal to the Chancellor because he exists, like God, only in an administrative vacuum.

Spinelli cannot remain. You, as a redoubtable fidei defensor, *know this, and also know that I will be at your side every step of the way as you renounce him as publicly and bloodily as you can.*

In Engineering, one of the first things I teach is the perfect unity of parts: nothing works without the co-operation of components, not a lawnmower, nor a poem, nor the internal combustion engine, nor a guided missile, nor the State. We have to be at one on this.

And beware; Spinelli is not a tyrant like others, he is more stupid, and is therefore, dangerous because the stupid only know how to hit out. So, once we have put him into the public domain, so to speak, guard your back, dear Frank.

For your edification, and which may be of use as information, these are some of the crimes associated with Spinelli:

*Eighteen political opponents executed without trial

*Mass execution of peasants (I have the photographs)

*Twenty-six accusations of rape

*Twenty-five corpses of rape accusers

*Two rigged elections

*CIA links to destroy democratic process – $500.000.000 in arms and supplies from the States

*Appointed three drug barons as Ministers

*250,000 political prisoners currently in prison

*Shares in profit from Pornography Empire

*Six hundred human rights violations

Yours truly, Roy.

"Yours Truly, Roy … Fish," said Jeremy Pickles aloud as he read the same memo, photocopied by one of the security guards, whose job it was to check and copy the mail of those the Registrar considered needed watching.

"Roy Fish, the bastard who bites the hand that feeds," said Pickles. Fish would be dealt with in good time. For the moment, he had to do something about Spinelli. He was sure Frank Finch lacked the spinach to publicly denounce Spinelli, and he'd get

Brimley to bully Finch into compliance, but Fish had an annoying habit of wanting the truth made public. It might be circumspect to keep the General out of sight for a while.

He looked out of the window and up at the Tower of Light. The Chancellor probably had a good idea something was amiss, but perhaps he didn't. Pickles never quite knew whether the Chancellor was completely removed from reality or frighteningly in tune with it.

He telephoned the General's suite of rooms in Bittermouth Universal House, and ten minutes later the little General entered in a plume of blue smoke, flanked by Boris and Boris. The General's vision of himself as the Wise Prophet had been put on hold by more pressing biological promptings.

"I iss very glad you call me thiss one time because I 'ave a leetle complaint, Meester Peekless."

"Ah. And what might that be, General?"

"There iss no wimmins. I hexpect you to be providing some wimmins for me, and maybe a few for Boris and Boris, maybe twins for them. Where iss my wimmins?"

"You mean prostitutes?" asked Pickles, instantly regretting it.

The General turned puce and rose up to his full five feet one and a half.

"Beleef me, Meester Peekless, I neffer pay. Wimmins are grateful to come to me for the – 'ow you say – shaftings of nookey rookey. Wimmins love power and when they are seeing me they know they 'as their 'ands on the rod of power," he said, his eyes becoming oily and menacing.

Pickles started to sweat.

"Of course. I meant … nothing at all. I'll see what I can do. In fact, it might be to the point as I was going to suggest that for a short while, a limited period, a merely transitory interlude, you move off campus and into an hotel. At no extra cost, of course. The Regal is an excellent place. Five star. Visiting royalty often stay there. Cuisine to die for … I mean to *live* for."

The General wasn't impressed.

"Wha' the fuck you say? You wanting mee to leef 'ere, after I pay you one big fuckings fortune?"

Pickles wished he had conducted this interview on the telephone. What if this psycho produced a gun or a knife or something?

"No, no. It was more your comfort we were considering. And the campus must be extremely tedious for you. I thought a change of scenery might inspire your studies."

"I am liking it 'ere. I stay. Why you so sweating wid drips? Something 'appens 'ere, I can sniffling it out. I know whens there iss a prob. You tell mee, Meester Peekless, whass wrong? And please don't lay, peoples who tell no truths to me are making mee very angry."

Boris and Boris stood stiffly behind him, watching. Something in Pickles' spine went Arctic and he knew he would have to tell the truth, which went against the administrative grain, but then he was usually dealing with people who were frightened of *him*.

"It's nothing, really, just that inevitably within the administrative and organizational structures of a complex and, I might say, highly innovative, educational institution, which is committed to targeting new growth areas and implementing review tools ..."

"Wha' the fuck you iss saying all this shitspeak 'ere, Peekless? I don' want to be 'earrings about your tool, juss spik the plain fuckings Quinn's Eenglish!" The General blew a large blue cumulus in Pickles' face. "I am one scholar 'ere, with thees illustrious Doctorr Feench, and you talking crap about I don't know whats."

"There is someone who objects to you being here, and I'm concerned he might make it difficult for us all," said Pickles.

"Who?"

"I can't possibly say."

"I hask one lass time. Who, Peekless?"

"Professor Roy Fish. Engineering."

"Hokay. And when you organise some wimmins – thees one first. Today."

The General threw down a photograph, then turned on his

miniature heels and was gone, along with the Boris twins. Only the stink of cigarillo smoke, a waft of spicy aftershave and the smell of his own fear remained.

Pickles looked at the photograph. There was no mistaking her. It was the big girl from the video, here sitting by the lake eating something and looking mournfully at the Canada Geese. The General clearly liked mountain women. Now he would have to find out who she was and talk to her. And could he really send her to Spinelli's suite in the full knowledge of what the General expected? It was going to be a difficult day.

And what if the General confronted Fish? There would be one hell of a row. He contemplated calling the Chancellor, but didn't want him to think he couldn't cope with what might turn out to be a very minor problem indeed. Or would the Chancellor be annoyed if he kept it to himself? Sometimes it was difficult to know what the man in the sky wanted.

Trev felt as if he was becoming unwired. It was only going to see Frank that made the world whole again; dangerous and unpredictable, but at least whole. On his own he felt things were coming apart and all sense of proportion deserted him. Worse were the moments when he lost all sense of himself as a warrior fighting for his love and felt he was a ragged little wisp shaved to bloody strips by jealousy. He discovered jealousy wasn't the green monster of folklore, but a thousand shards – anxieties, pains, questions – that destroyed concentration and made him remote to himself.

He watched himself walk to the kitchen and slap margarine on a medium-sliced white, then jam, and could feel someone's jaws munching miserably. Were they his? Of course they were, but they could have been anyone's. He saw someone mistily like himself climb into the bath and out again, gaze from the window, sigh deeply, dress and undress, dreamily but hideously real. The remoteness was itself a pain, a soul weariness of longing and ache. There was a gap somewhere in his solar plexus and at his worst moments he feared he would fall into it.

And here he was now, treading the library steps, with everything – the clip clop of heels, the banging of doors, the swish of electric fans, the ringing of mobile phones, the beep beep of electronic devices – somehow suggesting Damien Dimmuck and his beloved Cynth at it like amphetamised rabbits. How the clang of a cafeteria till downstairs or the cough of a pale librarian could suggest searing copulations, God alone knew, but they did, and he wondered: How often do they do it? Is he any good at it? How big is he? Does he talk to her while he's doing it? How long does it last for?

In his mind, Trev made list after list of the questions that multiplied and tortured him. He walked through the library and, even in his misery, noticed that each week there seemed to be fewer books and more people sitting in booths plugged into earphones and listening to Roebuck Learning Packages. He found a quiet corner and took out his copy of the *Aeneid.* He would force himself to concentrate.

An hour later he had read the whole of Books Five and Six, and something galvanised.

Ah! child of tears! Can'st thou again be free
And burst Fate's cruel bondage ...

Fate's cruel bondage. That's what all this is about. Some great unknown and indifferent force playing out its hand, with him, little Trev, tossed like a twig in its tides. But the heroes didn't just accept this – they fought on anyway, even if the odds were hopeless. And that is what he, Trevor Bottom, beloved of Cynth, would do. You had to fight even if you couldn't win; otherwise what was the point? You may just as well curl up and die. And you certainly couldn't go on to become a great writer if you were dead, although paradoxically most of the great writers are dead. You did the writing, dropped dead, then people called you great.

He also found something in the front of the book – an inscription to himself from Doctor Finch: *My Dear Boy, there is an old Chinese proverb: It is better to light one candle than curse the darkness. Sincerely, Frank Finch.* That did it.

He wasn't going to lie down and wallow. He would go forth

and wallow. He would do something while wallowing. He decided that the best place to go was into the enemy's camp. He'd light a candle rather than curse the darkness.

Chapter Twenty-Seven

Jeremy Pickles was amazed. He'd summoned the fat student girl to his office and she'd waddled in, sat down, and he'd said she'd been chosen by a special sub-committee for inter-racial harmony enhancement to meet a visiting foreign PhD student as a gesture of Roebuck hospitality and the raising of cultural awareness and international empathy. He said it would go on her personal file that she had made a significant contribution to multicultural understanding and cross-fertilization.

The word "fertilization" had perhaps been a little ill-considered, as had "raising", but at least he'd avoided the word "penetration". She just seemed to accept it all, took the address and time, and left. In fact, now he came to think about it, he could swear she hadn't said a single word throughout. God, if only the academics could be like that.

Cynth walked across Bittermouth Plaza, a huge concrete rectangle the size of four football pitches and with the figure of Icarus etched in mosaic on the flagstones at its centre, so if you saw it from a helicopter it looked as if a huge bird had been squashed flat by a giant cosmic boot.

The Plaza separated student accommodation from a cluster of palatial buildings, one of which was Bittermouth Universal House.

High up in Bittermouth Tower, Adam zoomed in on Cynth and wondered why she was walking towards Universal House – she didn't look like Universal House material in her faded jeans and loose white smock, bobbed hair and depressed air. It was odd also because students, especially the girl variety, usually roved in packs.

God, she needs to drop some weight, otherwise gravity will get her sooner rather than later, he thought with a shiver. Already she seems weighed down, burdened by something. It was strange, too, how being above and removed from the world gave you a perspicacity, something almost omniscient, he thought. And an old quotation bubbled into his mind: "A woman moved is like a fountain troubled. Muddy, ill-seeming, thick, bereft of beauty." A sudden and alarming memory flash of Rosemary Puddock's breasts thumping into his face made him shiver and he changed the screen to see what was happening in the Roebuck Sports Emporium, formerly the gym.

Cynth didn't know why she had agreed to meet this foreign student. Actually she didn't agree, she simply took the address and time: 7:30pm. People mistook silence for complicity. She had discovered that silence was an enormous space in which people projected their own longings and meanings, and which had nothing to do with her. It was now seven twenty-five. The truth, she realised, was that she was going because she didn't care. One thing was as good as another. Everything was the same. She was going to listen to someone. It didn't really matter who it was or what he said.

Her poems had gone – she knew she wouldn't get them back now. The Creative Writing tutor had probably lost them or shoved them in a drawer and would never bother to retrieve them. It was another thing that didn't matter really. Somehow sleep had become more real to her than waking – it didn't matter what happened during the day.

Her dreams were all about Dad now, and she realised she could no longer distinguish what had actually happened when he had been there and what happened in the dream world. They would talk for hours; they would go on special trips together – Kew gardens, Charlecote Manor, Norfolk where they had their few family holidays, the little dog called Scramble yapping excitedly at her first sight of the sea – and there would be lots of laughter; quiet discussions about life, love, the future; books he would tell her to read; his eyes brown and starting to crow-foot at the corners. Now she couldn't honestly say what of this was the actual lived past and what was the stuff of her dreams. Both were real in some way she didn't understand.

Perhaps all history was imagined. The dead live on in us, they go wherever we take them, including our dreams, she thought. They have no choice. They cannot leave us a second time.

Boris opened the door and Boris stood just behind him. Cynth had seen them around the campus. They both bowed slightly and then showed her into a huge living room that overlooked the lake. It had a Persian carpet of swirling patterns that shone like silk, and four leather sofas. On the wall were the skins of animals – a tiger, two lions, a bear and a few things she didn't recognize. She had read that primitive hunters thought they took on the energy and spirit of an animal they killed, but here in a modern room it seemed ridiculous. And a small tank or something had probably killed these beasts. No risk.

A cough made her realise there was someone in the room, a small man, almost hidden by a large vase of coloured grasses. He exhaled a blue plume of smoke at the window then approached Cynth, his teeth glittering off-whitely.

He wore a gold military jacket with red epaulettes and a row of medals, so long that it looked like a large multicoloured centipede was clinging to his chest.

Women and uniforms. The General wanted to impress, first with his military stature, then with his intellect, and finally with his sexual prowess.

"Senora, iss my pleasure. Iss a 'onours you comings to my leetle rooms in this one fine seats of learnings. And what I am haskings you study? No, let me guess? Iss something beautiful, yess? Hart? I 'ave many hart paintings in my 'ouse at 'ome – original Picassoles and Dellis, all gifts to me by grateful hassociates. Now you like this one drink – Margarita?"

Cynth saw a glass bowl of exquisite looking chocolates. She thought of Ely Cathedral, the sacred, terrible tin. Spinelli registered the look.

"Ah yess, for the ladies iss the sweets tooths. 'Elp-a-yourself," he said, holding out the bowl.

She took a chocolate mint in the shape of a gun and a white chocolate in the shape of a rosebud. They were delicious. If only he would leave the room, she could stuff a handful in her pocket.

Spinelli looked at Boris and Boris. They read his eyes and were gone. They had things to do.

"Now we can get – 'ow you say – properly acquainteded," said Spinelli, indicating one of the sofas.

Cynth sat and the leather squeaked as she sank into its softness. The General sat next to her, still smiling.

"You know I am a PhD, I do this one transerlation of the Aeneid. My supervisor 'e is saying eet iss radical. Maybe I give up my job and be one full time scholars. Then I could be meetings with the beautiful girls like you. Ha ha! And maybe, later, I read you my transerlations. 'Ow you say – giving them a damn good herring."

Chapter Twenty-Eight

Trev Bottom knocked on Damien's door, waited for a moment, and entered. He had no real plan. He just wanted to find further evidence of the affair, and perhaps clues to its intensity, and then act from there. He knew it would cause him more pain and there would be a price to pay in list making, but jealousy is a cruel taskmaster, one which demands the sufferer seek out that which will torment him most.

There was a smell of aftershave. He looked around the untidy room. Coffee cups and papers littered most surfaces. It was odd being in the room without Damien himself and the other Creative Writing students. On the desk he read part of a letter offering Damien a job in California as Professor of Creative Writing, "… *What most impressed us were the poems from your forthcoming book. They were extraordinary and will doubtless be an enormous success. Particularly good were* 'Watching You Leave' *and* 'Cloud Messages', *though all were stunning …*" So Damien might be leaving. The sooner the better. But would Cynth go with him?

He looked in the filing cabinet: mostly university admin, a lot of half finished poems on scraps of paper. He looked through the desk drawer and found a photograph turned face down of a tired looking young woman and a chubby, rather ugly, little boy with a pout and Damien's flattish nose, who was obviously refusing steadfastly to smile for the camera. Then he saw and recognised it at once. He'd seen her carry that pink folder. He lifted it out. On the front it simply said POEMS and beneath that the treasured name C. Blake. She had actually given Damien her poems – what greater evidence of intimacy could there be? C. Blake. Written with her own sweet hand. The hand that had touched Damien.

C. Blake. One day, when all the turmoil and agony of this grim time had been buried beneath a welter of passion and forgiveness, she would write that name in the marriage register, watched by a smiling lady registrar with bright red lipstick who wished Cynth and Trev lifelong happiness. (No church wedding – Trev was an atheist. Cynth would understand that he couldn't compromise his principles.) Flowers and champagne – only two glasses if he was driving. No friends and relatives to ruin things, this was to be an intensely private and joyous occasion. The Yorkshire terriers would be waiting in the car – something a bit bohemian, like a Renault Clio with its risqué associations of France and illicit love. Then they'd be off to start their new life by the seaside.

Then … oh shit, someone was coming in. Trev dived under the desk and hid in the shadows behind the waste bin. He noticed a whiff of unpleasantness from it, which obviously had something to do with an ancient banana, dozens of snotty tissues and a sock.

He saw two pairs of legs enter, one pair was Damien's with that mincing walk, as if his bum was pouting, and the other pair belonged to Helen. Those shapely ankles – forgive me, darling Cynth – were unmistakable. He hoped they'd go soon as he was cramped and his head was against the radiator, which was full on and his right ear was already painfully hot. He could hear something gurgling far off. Could it be music?

"Great to see the new draft, Helen, it's really coming on. I mean that. There's a sort of dynamic in it that wasn't there before. I always knew you had this kind of inner intensity; it's just a question of transferring that into your writing. It came to me early, but hey … you're getting there too. Fabulous. We'll go through it later. How about a drink first? End of the day. Cocktail hour. I could do with one."

"A'right. I'll have a beer," said Helen.

"Only wine, I'm afraid. Chardonnay. Quite pleasant."

"A'right."

Pop. Slosh. Gurgle.

Trev's ear was pink. Christ, if they start drinking they could be here for hours. He'd seen Helen in the Bittermouth Lounge knocking back pint after pint. She could drink for England, and then some.

"So you're enjoying the course, then?" asked Damien, sitting down and patting the seat next to him. Trev could see his bum as he swung the chair close to Helen's.

"'S'alreet. I mean, yeah. A lot of me mates are, like, dead jealous they couldn't get on it."

"It is very popular, but I have to be selective. You were a dead cert, though. I knew that straight off," said Damien.

"'Ow come? I mean, you didn't know if I could write or nowt."

"Call it instinct."

Slosh gurgle slosh.

They were knocking it back quickly enough. Trev managed to move slightly just as his ear was about to explode. Now the back of his head was against the radiator.

"There was just something about you," said Damien. "I find you intriguing."

"Why's that then?"

Slosh. Gurgle. Slosh.

"Just a sort of aura about you. Plus you're very attractive, but you must know that."

"Me Ma says I got an arse like a donkey's."

"Hardly. You have classical features. And amazing eyes. I started a poem about you the other day. I'll read it to you later. Have some more. I've got another bottle."

Slosh. Gurgle. Slosh.

He saw Damien's hand move and put itself on Helen's.

"I've been wondering all term what it would be like to kiss you," said Damien.

Oh buggery bollocks, thought Trev. If he starts humping her what'll I do? I might be sick in the bin. He tried to tell himself that all experiences were good for a writer, but he could instantly think of lots he'd rather do without: being in a road accident and losing a limb; having maggots put in your underpants; being raped by a Glaswegian stoker; dying of starvation; having a large spot on the end of your nose on your wedding night; athlete's foot; being probed my mad scientists. They were just a few and having to watch and listen to his Creative Writing tutor humping Helen over the desk with him beneath and his head boiling was definitely up there with those. In fact, making mental lists of all the most horrible Room 101 things that could happen to him might be the only way to survive this ordeal.

"So, do you mind if I kiss you?"

"A bit," said Helen. "I mean, you're already … you know."

"Already married. Yes, but it's a complicated story. My wife knows I have expansive desires. Being a writer. It's a question of chemistry and she understands that. I mean – between you and me – there's a sort of electricity. You must feel it too."

Trev wanted to vomit. His hair was starting to singe too, so he moved an inch or two and put his other ear against the radiator. Did Damien say all this stuff to Cynth the first time they …? It was too horrible to contemplate.

"It's nowt to do with your wife. It's just that you're already well up to it with one lass in the group, and I s'pose I'd like to have been first, like. To show respect."

"What are you talking about?"

Cynth, Cynth, she's talking about the love of my life, thought Trev miserably.

"Everyone knows. We've all seen it. Whole bloody campus's seen it," said Helen.

"Seen what?"

"You and her. At it. In the lift. We've all seen the video, over and bloody over again. On campus TV. Must have been a security tape or something. Unless you set it up, kinky like. Some blokes love all that. "

A large penny dropped in Damien's mind. There's a security camera in the lift. But surely whoever operated it wouldn't show it on campus TV unless … that bitch must have something to do with it. She ensnares me in the lift, gets the tape, then has it broadcast all over Roebuck to prove she'd been with me, to force me into some sort of relationship. Women were so devious, so conniving, so manipulative.

"So thanks for the drink but I got to go. Meetin' some mates. And cheers for lookin' at me story." Helen left the room and closed the door. There was a moment's silence.

"Stupid fat bitch!" Damien shouted, startling Trev so that he banged his head on the desk.

"Bitch bitch bitch bitch bitch!"

Trev felt he should leap out and confront Damien for calling the love of his life a bitch, but in a way it wasn't a bad thing because it might mean it would all be over between them and the way forward would be free for Trev. His thoughts were disturbed by a thump above him. What the hell was going on? Damien had jumped on the desk. What was he doing?

Moments later his shoes were thrown on the floor, then his trousers, then his Y-fronts. What the hell was he doing? A low moan provided the answer. No, please God. No. I don't want to be here while he's having a whack on the desk above me. It's obscene, thought Trevor. How do I get into these situations? And maybe calling his beloved Cynth a fat bitch was some sort of trigger for sex, a perverse way of getting himself worked up. Dirty talk. Perhaps she even liked it. Please God, no. Please … No … No … No …

The desk started to rock and Trev tried to blank out what was happening by listing in his mind the awful things he would like to happen to Damien: a large beetle crawls into his ear and starts to eat its way through, dropping eggs and little beetley turds on the way; he is somehow utterly humiliated in front of everyone he had ever known; his internal organs all catch fire. It was no good, the moans were getting louder.

"Yes, yes, do it to me, baby. Oh, you're so ripe. Oh Damien, I want your hotness all over me. Oh, Da-mi-en … Yes baby, it's all for you …"

Trev tried to remember quotations: *Do not presume too much upon my love; I may do that I shall be sorry for.*

"Oh Dame, I want it, I want it!"

"It is better to light one candle than to curse the darkness."

"I'm mad for it, baby!"

"Though this be madness. Yet there is method in it."

"I love your cock!"

"Hickory Dickory Dock."

"You're so hot, baby, like fire. Scald me. Yes, yes, scald me!"

"I am bound upon a wheel of fire that mine own tears do scald like molten lead."

"I love you doing that to me*!"*

"With love too much, hate in the like extreme."

"Come on now, come on big boy!"

"The rain in Spain stays mainly on the plain."

"Yes! Yes! Ohhhh Damien!"

"Oh shit."

Damien lay panting on the desk and Trev sat beneath, nursing his burnt ears and frizzed hair. Every limb ached. He felt part of his mind become detached and float away. A crumpled tissue was thrown from the desk onto the floor. Trev sat in a pool of darkening misery until he heard snuffling snores from the desk above. He extricated himself, rubbed some circulation back into his legs then crept from the room, carrying C. Blake's pink folder of poems.

High up in the Bittermouth Tower of Light the Chancellor stared at the screen. The image of the masturbating frolics on the desk and the strange hunched little figure that had crept beneath it confirmed that he was best out of it. Clearly sexual practices had become so exhausted that these people had sunk to new depths of dissoluteness to rekindle their jaded appetites. The sooner he could get rid of people altogether from his university, the safer and cleaner he and the campus would be.

Chapter Twenty-Nine

Brimley began to wonder if it was such a good idea after all.

However, the fact that it had now been eight days and three hours and twenty-two minutes (we measure our lives with our preoccupations) gave him no choice. And Nora was so reassuring, almost like a second mother, except better than his own mater because she didn't make him tidy his room and humiliate him in front of his friends by telling them he couldn't go out to play because of his weak chest, weak eyes and weak bladder. Nora was just patiently, dependably there. And he could have occasional sex with her if he felt like it.

He sat and watched as she quietly unrolled and prepared black tubes, transparent tubes, what looked like a medieval demijohn, a few jars and bottles and little bits of equipment he would rather not know about. Let her take over. Just, please God, let it work.

She spread a blanket on his desk and, rather self consciously considering she did know him carnally, he undressed and lay on it face down. He closed his eyes.

"Just relax," she said, smiling.

"Shouldn't we have some sort of signal, in case I want you to stop?" asked Brimley.

"How about saying, 'Stop, Nora'," she said.

Sarcasm was not Nora's domain. Nora did not speak like that. Perhaps it was because she was concentrating.

"Just relax," she said, and he tried to think soothing thoughts: watching Frank squirm when he threatened him with dismissal; putting Damien in his place; the eight or so people he'd had the pleasure of sacking during his professional life. He felt something being slipped around his wrists, oh so gently, then his ankles, like butterfly touches.

"Think pleasant thoughts," she said.

As he felt something slip inside him, he imagined Ronald Drain being garrotted by brutal women in Nazi uniforms. He thought of one day being a Pro-Vice Chancellor, of running the whole CRAP project himself. One day he might actually get to meet the Chancellor, and be invited to the top of the Tower of Light for sherry and scheming. He thought of a life without constipation. Such were his dreams, a small naked man plugged with tubes.

Actually it wasn't at all unpleasant. There was a bit of gurgling then he felt a rush of warm water. This was fine, a piece of cake. It was going to work. Nora was utterly in control. He felt warm breath on his face and opened his eyes. Nora was bending down, her face close to his. She looked different. The smile wasn't a Nora smile. It belonged to someone cooler, someone more remote, someone he found alarming.

"Now," she said, "tell me why you lied to me."

"I haven't," he replied automatically and, for a second, thought Nora really was his mother and he'd been caught with his hand in the biscuit barrel.

"Oh dear, let's try again. Why did you tell me your wife was going away for the weekend when she wasn't, and why did you lie to me about it again afterwards?"

"Nora, you've got it all wrong. She did go away but she came back early. I'm sorry if I didn't explain that more clearly." He tried to turn over, but realised his hands and feet were tied to the desk. What the cat-crapping hell was going on?

"No. She never was going away. Look at me, Brimley." She leaned close to him, and he realised for the first time she had violet eyes. He could have sworn they were blue or brown or something.

"What does it matter? Untie me now and take that bloody contraption out of my arse!" Brimley thought a little assertiveness might break this strange mood.

"Shut up, Brimley, and listen," she said calmly. "For eighteen months I have been there for you entirely on your terms. In my own quiet, unobtrusive way I fell in love with you. I accepted that I was something to be filed away, a convenience, and that your real life was elsewhere. I knew you never thought about or considered me. All that was fine, if only you had just told me the truth occasionally."

"Ha!" shouted Brimley, trying to fight a sense of rising hysteria.

"Why is it so much to ask? Why is it necessary to dissemble at every turn, when it doesn't matter anyway," Nora asked.

"Because human relationships are like that. You don't tell people the truth, for God's sake. Life would be impossible. Don't you understand that yet, you cretinous little woman," said Brimley, instantly regretting it. "Nora, I'm sorry, I didn't mean that. I do respect you, honestly, and I did think that one day you and I ..."

"Don't! You were just beginning to get somewhere. You do think I'm a cretin. Then you pull back and insult my intelligence with a lot of lying twaddle. You think only of what you want. Have you never considered that I might have dreams?"

"Well ..." Of course he had never considered such a thing. Why should he?

"That I might want to be a wife and mother? Or an exotic mistress in a jewelled thong and feather boa. Or a *femme fatale* in a red cocktail dress and with a loaded gun in my bag?"

"What the bloody hell are you talking about? You're mad!"

"No, I'm human. That's all." Tears glistened in her eyes.

"Nora, let's stop all this. Pretend it never happened. Let's go out for a meal, well perhaps just a drink, a quick one, then ..."

"Yes, you need a drink, Brimley. You need to loosen up. It's what you've always needed."

"What do you mean?"

Nora took a half bottle of gin and a half bottle of vodka from her irrigation bag. She poured the vodka into the glass jar from which warm water was steadily gurgling into Brimley.

"Cheers," said Nora. "Here's to all the little celebrations we never had. Bottoms up." Then she poured in the gin. "I'd love to stay but Mother's peptic ulcer is playing up and I have to prepare the Complan. The cleaners will be around in about two hours. And you won't see me again. I quit."

"Nora! For Pity's sake, Nora. Don't go. I'll give you a salary raise. There's this project, CRAP. I'll give you a percentage. Nora!"

But she had gone. And there was a searing pain deep in his bowel. All hell was letting loose in there. Desert Storm had replaced constipation.

"Aagh! Nora! Please, I'll do anything! We'll get married. It's what I always wanted. Oh Jesus, it hurts, oh Sweet Fucking Mary, it hurts. Help!"

His eyes streamed, self-pity welled, he felt quite drunk already but even that did not anaesthetise the bloody and crippling agony. He felt as if his insides had been blasted with a blowtorch. The cleaners would come and find him. He would intimidate them into keeping quiet about this, or perhaps bribe them, but he couldn't wait for hours. He might be dead by then. He needed help. Medical help. Now.

Adam Bittermouth watched his large digital screen and shook his head in consternation and horror. His Professor of Quality Assurance in English seemed to be in great agony, yet he had willingly undressed and allowed that woman to do unspeakable things to him.

Perhaps the whole of Roebuck was in the thrall of some fetishising epidemic. He was Chancellor of a sick and degenerate academic population, an amoral empire of dying wasps turning upon itself, and he was Nero fiddling in the Tower of Light while his world went to hell around him. Human beings were the most revolting creatures in the universe. He felt a tremor and looked up. Had the ceiling lowered a little? Was the Dark Invader, master of gravity, even now on the roof?

He telephoned his Academic Registrar.

"Pickles, I want more security guards. I want them to arrest anyone behaving antisocially."

"But Chancellor, Sir, neither they nor we have the legal power to do that," said Pickles.

"Why do we have a Law Department if not to help us maintain

order?"

"I'll see what I can do, Sir. It may be that under the terms and conditions of citizen's arrest we could argue something. I could telephone the Police Commissioner too, a blind eye to any complaints – perhaps if I mentioned an honorary degree at next year's awards?"

"Whatever it takes," said the Chancellor.

In his office Brimley could bear it no longer. He was both helplessly drunk and in mortal agony, bathed in cold sweat and excrement. He turned his head and managed to stretch so that his nose could just about reach the telephone. He banged it down on the exchange button and wailed in pain.

"Roebuck University, how may I help you?" said a young female voice.

"Need help. Medical help," gasped Brimley, finding ordinary speech difficult because he was in enormous pain and completely ratted.

"I'm sorry. This is Roebuck University, not a hospital."

"I know issa fucking university!" shouted Brimley.

"I'm sorry, but we have a zero tolerance policy towards abuse of exchange staff. I'll have to hang up."

"No no, don't hang up, pleash. I jush meant I work here. I am ashally here now."

"Then why don't you dial the internal number you want? It's in your directory."

"I can't look in my directory, I'm ... tied up."

"Then how can I help?"

"As I shtarted by shaying *(don't be rude to her)* I need medical help *(you dull-witted bimbo)* ... if you'd be so good, with heartsh and flowersh all pretty pretty pleash thank you very much."

"What exactly is wrong with you? You sound sort of drunk."

"Am short of drunk. Pretty fucking obvious, I'd shay."

"We have a zero tolerance policy towards drunken abuse of exchange staff. I'm going to have to ..."

"No no, pleash don't. I wash made drunk by a woman. Against

my will. When I wash naked."

"If it's sexual harassment, then don't you want the Roebuck Counsellor and Legal Aid Operative?"

"No, no," said Brimley, weeping with misery. "I want a doctor. I have been tied up and had a great big thingy tube thing shtuck up my arsh and gin and vodka shloshed up it until I'm in ekshtreme pain and I might die and I want to finish my bloody awful book that I hate before I die and I've made a mesh everywhere but ish not my fault do you unnershtand?"

But she had already located where the call was coming from, hung up and called security. Five minutes later the uniformed Baz and Dave arrived. Dave knocked on the door, tried the handle, then Baz opened it with his master key. They both came in and Dave held his nose against the stench while Baz took in the scene.

"Fuckin' 'ell, Baz, smells like a bleedin' karzy at a pop festival. What's that perv doin' bollock naked d'you reckon?" said Dave.

Baz approached Brimley.

"So, in a spot of bother, are we? In a bit of a pickle? A postmodern seminar on bondage that went a bit too far, was it? No, don't tell me – a workshop on erotic plumbing. Am I getting close?"

"'Shnot my fault. Victim. Gemme doctor." Brimley's face had gone purple.

"Drunk in charge of a stationery desk. Very serious charge, that is," said Baz. "Defacing, not to say defecating on, university property. Says Professor of Quality Assurance on your door. Now my question to you is: do you really think this sets a good example of rarefied intellectual life to the young? What do you think, Dave?"

"Def'nitely not, Baz. Def'nitely not. I'd say 'e's a shirt-lifting bondage perv. I mean you only gotta look. Disgusting 'ow am I gonna eat me vindaloo after this lot without some serious upchuck?"

"Gemme doctor now, you stupid little Nazi!" Brimley knew even before the sentence was out that it was another huge mistake.

"Tut-tut. Language," said Baz. "Have you ever heard the like, Dave? And from a professor and all?"

Dave shook his head.

"Never in all my. I mean what the fuck's the world coming to? A professor turns out not only a perv that shouldn't be allowed near young minds, but a fucking foul mouthed cunt as well. Makes me sick, Baz."

"You've got to help me. Ish not fair," said Brimley, snot and tears all over his face. "I'll report you to the Registrar."

"Yeh? But I'm not the cunt lying there with a tube up his arse, am I, Professor? So you report me to who you like. That is, when you manage to Houdini your way out of this knotty little problem," said Baz, heading for the door.

"Nice one, Bazza," said Dave, joining him. "These bleedin' academics speak through their arses so they might as well drink through 'em as well, I s'pose."

The door closed behind their laughter and Brimley wished he were dead. And a lot of other people too.

Chapter Thirty

Roy Fish knew there was something wrong even before it happened.

As he came out of the lift on the eighth floor of the car park and walked towards his Toyota, his heels echoing, he sensed he wasn't alone. Years of intelligent ferreting, pursued hunches and logical investigation had equipped him with radar that rarely let him down. It was seven o'clock and there were few cars, apart from his, before the evening Bittermouth Arts Centre rush. A battered Mazda and an expensive four wheel drive USV, as people whose idea of sport is to go shopping in a tank called them.

Something was wrong. You can't watch a watcher without him knowing. He could go back to the lift. He could get to his car, jump in and drive off as quickly as possible. But he was Roy Fish. He did things in his own way and at his own pace. He beeped the security locks on his car, and as he reached forward to open the door, they were there.

"Good evening. How can I help you?" he asked, turning to face Boris, who gave the ghost of a smile and nodded at Boris who was standing the other side of Fish. This Boris put an arm around Fish's neck, tightened it, twisted and his neck snapped. He convulsed and twitched a little, and Boris held him firm until it was all over. It took less than a minute. They carried his body as if it were a puppet to the edge of the car park and threw it over, where it ragtaggled through the air and landed with a thump in the rhododendrons fifty feet below.

Then Boris the first went to each of the four CCTV cameras and took the tape off the lens, and crab-walked against the walls and out of shot, back to Bittermouth Universal House. It was a pleasant evening. Quiet. If either had talked, they would have said to each other what a fine evening it was for a stroll.

As they strolled Frank sat in his office reading a memo from Brimley:

> *Dear Dr Finch, it has come to my attention*
> *that you have received a letter from Dr Roy*
> *Fish regarding the PhD student Vittorio*
> *Spinelli. The letter is a scurrilous attack on*
> *the student. Further, there are procedures for*
> *making   complaints,   and   private*
> *correspondence is not part of that process.*
> *Dr Fish is an ambitious man, and may have*
> *his own agenda. In any case, the Registrar*
> *and I have no doubt you will disregard the*
> *contents, especially as they may involve you*
> *in litigation. The worst-case scenario is*
> *dismissal for bringing the university into*
> *disrepute.*
>
> *Yours etc, Professor Brimley Trevalyan.*

By the time he had finished reading it, Boris and Boris arrived back at General Spinelli's apartment and, had they possessed the capacity for surprise, this would have been the moment for it. No weeping battered girl, no impotent rages from the General, and no nasty mess for them to dispose of. The girl sat on the sofa watching and listening as the General, deliriously happy, marched up and down declaiming his avant-garde radical translation:

"'Scarce 'ad this one Rosie rais'd 'er 'ead

Above this chief's rod in 'er steamings bed.'.

"You see, then 'e is puttings all these things he taked from those bastards 'e is killing. Iss like a trophies, comprendez? 'E one great champione. You like? I like because this Virgil says if peoples are fucking you off and you are 'aving to –'ow you say – making the jaw bones crack and they knees go slack, then you got to take their stuff as well. Iss the trophies of war!"

He stopped marching up and down and turned to Boris and Boris. His face was flushed, like a schoolboy who'd won his first race.

"This wimmins, she my queen. She my one best wimmins. Why you find me no mores like these? I telling you. Because she iss the honly one. She leesten to me. She unnerstand me. She know my soul like no wimmins hevver. And – you knows what – she don't say one fucking words. S'cuzez, Cherie, (*a small respectful and apologetic nod at Cynth*). Because I tell you why – she don' need to always be with the speakings like them whores always wanting geefts and jewels and crap jus' because they 'ave the 'onours of my fucking them big time. S'cuzez, my angel.

"I 'onour this wimmins. I swear on this graves of my mother I will never lay my fingers all over 'er until we iss mens and wifes. I, Vittorio Carbella Vincentio Carlos Juanta Manuel Spinelli, do swear this one oaths with you as my whitenesses."

Boris and Boris stared impassively. If they were moved by this proposal of marriage, it didn't show.

Spinelli prattled on for another five minutes, declaiming the infinite depths and virtues of Cynth. She sat and listened and felt the call of Ely Cathedral, the silence of her room, the dreams where she wandered in hope of finding her dad. This ridiculous little man, whoever he was, and his absurd prattle, seemed to be in another world. She stood when he paused for breath and moved towards the door.

"Yess, I know. You are overcoming with thees feelings too. Until tomorrow, my little – 'ow you say – dumplings. My love has no bottoms."

He even followed her down to the door and, as she stepped out into Bittermouth Plaza, he took a wad of twenty pound notes from his pocket and stuffed them down her blouse.

"You are buyings somethings beeootiful for yourselfs. Maybe some underwearings. Wimmins like all this panties and thongs I know. You are coming tomorrow same time and I am telling you many theengs about myselfs and read my transerlations many times. We be so 'appy like bins in this one pod, like snugs in the rugs of bugs. Iss good?"

And he blew little spittled kisses at her as she ambled slowly across the square, already anticipating the safety of her room, and something else. A sense that an unnameable immensity had turned in her, wearily and inevitably, like a piece of machinery winding down to its inexorable close.

As he hugged her poems to his breast and watched from the shadow of Icarus, his heart stilled and frozen by what he had seen and heard – the gift of money, the intimacy, the declaration of love, the blown kisses – the world suddenly seemed huge and insurmountable to Trevor Bottom. Another rival … this dwarfish loudmouthed man. For Christ's sake, how many others did she have stowed away? He was just getting used to Damien and plotting his destruction, when now there was another one. Suppose there were so many he would have to make a list of them?

For a moment he wavered and thought how much simpler life would be without her and the attendant complications, but his heart unfolded and he remembered the terriers, the house by the sea, the racy little Renault, the lock of hair on her forehead, the postcoital bliss of cups of tea and sweaty sheets.

He had also started to read her poems that afternoon, and they were painfully good, and if possible, made her more desirable. The conversations they could have about writing. He couldn't help himself. The battle would go on. It was love, and however much he struggled against it, he was still in its thrall.

She had taken money from that man. Perhaps she had been forced into prostitution, or maybe he had her hooked on drugs. Somehow that was preferable to thinking she did these things with other men of her own volition. Whatever it was, he, Trev, would be her salvation.

Chapter Thirty-One

The cleaners had argued at first. When they entered Brimley's room and found him crying and gibbering, still tied to the desk, the room a cesspool of filth and stink and squalor, Madge had wanted to bludgeon him to death with her bucket, but Bren insisted on calling the doctor.

"He's sick," she said.

"Too bloody right he is. What we do is kill the pervert then call the police and say it was self defence," said Madge, whose view of men had not changed since her husband left her for a pole dancer in Wolverhampton.

"How can it be self defence when he's tied up and trolleyed out of his brains?"

"We could bludgeon the bastard to death then untie him and say he attacked us in an entirely unprovoked fashion," countered Madge.

"But that would be murder," said Bren.

"Your point being what, exactly?"

"Let's just call the doctor," said Bren.

Calling the doctor was fine, but now that Dr Duff had arrived, carrying a new Prince racquet and in his starched tennis whites, getting him to enter the room was proving more difficult. The three of them stood outside Brimley's door. Dr Duff listened and heard a whimper from inside.

"You say there appears to be human excrement in there?" he asked them for the third time, holding a eucalyptus-soaked tissue to his mouth and nose.

"We don't know it's human," said Madge enigmatically. "But it's everywhere."

"Then I can't possibly go in. I know what you're thinking.

Human faeces are only undigested residues, water and secretions, but you'd be wrong. My God you'd be labouring under the mother of all delusions there. There are also bacteria. That room is now a laboratory of disease, a playground for stercoblin, created by bacterial action of bilirubin. Have you any idea how many billion parasitical microbes are now breeding copiously in there, ready to hook any poor passing victim into their dance of death?"

Madge shook her head. Bren wondered if she should call security. The doctor had a wild look in his eye and he was chopping the air with his racquet as he spoke.

"I'd say something in the region of seventy-six billion. And that's being conservative. They are escaping under the door even as we speak. Trichiuris trichiura and cyclospora ready to ambush; cryptosporidium and strongyloides stercoralis plotting our downfall in a secret microlanguage we could not decode in a thousand years."

Madge looked down at her feet in alarm and started to scratch her head. The whole world was starting to feel infected.

Dr Duff narrowed his eyes suspiciously as new dreams of death and disease washed over him.

"You say he has a tube in his rectum?" he asked.

"No, it's stuck up his arse," said the now terrified Madge.

"Then I'm afraid there are more possibilities we should face," said the doctor.

Bren knew by now he was completely mad, but Madge seemed to be caught in the bacterial web the doctor was weaving.

"We have to face the possibility of coprophagia," he said, shaking his head.

Madge took a sharp intake of breath. She had no idea what he was talking about, but his expression made her think of zombies and slashers and wriggling offal oozing from ghoulish aliens.

"What's that?"

"The extremely hazardous practice of being sexually attracted to faeces and eating them."

Madge felt sick and had to swallow hard and think of pink roses to keep her from throwing up over the doctor's pristine whites.

"And then there's the effusion of gases, the maelstrom of flatulence that can cause worldwide disasters."

"What are you talking about?" asked Bren.

"Hitler. Adolf Hitler. That's what I'm talking about."

"You mean that weirdo in there is Hitler?" Bren felt her wits deserting her.

"No, but we may be entering a similar worldwide catastrophe. Hitler suffered from terrible flatulence. He was treated by Dr Theodore Morell, who prescribed Dr Koster's anti-gas pills, which contained a mixture of strychnine and belladonna, plus the infamous 'golden tablets' containing large amounts of caffeine and the highly addictive amphetamine pervitin. As you know, the latter causes disorientation and hallucination. This is the explanation for Hitler's schizophrenia, his impaired and reckless judgement, and his megalomania.

"And there you have it – the Second World War, the Holocaust, millions of deaths, all because of breaking wind. A chilling thought, that a fart can almost end civilization as we know it, but true. So you see, what awaits us in there is too apocalyptic, too dangerous, to even consider entering."

A drunken, burping moan came from inside the room.

"But he needs a doctor," said Bren.

"No, my dear woman. What he needs is a damned good plumber and a dozen storm troopers in case he gets nasty." The doctor had recovered some composure and was practising a backhand volley. "And now, if you'll excuse me, I have a floodlit doubles on court number three to attend to. I need a few minutes to perfect my second slice serve."

He walked off whistling *Edelweiss*.

Chapter Thirty-Two

Trevor sat miserably contemplating what to do. He heard an ambulance siren on the campus ring road and half-heartedly wondered whom it was for.

In fact it was taking the now cold body of Roy Fish to the hospital. Trevor hoped it might be for Damien. He hoped that Damien had got his head trapped in the lift door and that the lift had hurtled right up to the fifth floor and now his decapitated trunk was on its way to the morgue. More likely, though, he was drinking a glass of white wine before shafting another First Year, or whacking off and screaming his own name at the crucial moment. Or getting ready to see Cynth. After all she'd left the loud little South American pretty early – it was only eight thirty. And now the thought had been planted he had to know. The jealous cannot leave their open sores alone. The desire to know is their downfall.

Trevor felt there was something noble in his desire to take a full look at the worst. In his failed attempt to write a Shakespeare essay that morning, the lines from Henry V1 part 2 had struck him as both true and now, given what he'd just witnessed, ominous: "True nobility is exempt from fear. More can I bear than you dare execute." It meant only one thing. He had to be there, to face things. He could take it. And if he still won her, despite two rivals who were older and worldlier, it would prove he was the better man. It would be his rite of passage. Trevor the Steadfast. In years to come, the terriers at their feet, they would laugh at this, and Cynth would say for the thousandth time that it was as if she had never been kissed until Trev's lips were pressed fully against hers. If he ran through the Student Union and past Bittermouth Book Centre he could easily get to Cynth's hall before she did.

When he arrived he tried her door, which was locked, as he

feared it would be. He waited in the communal kitchen. No one was there as the kitchen was only used for all night drinking sessions once the bars had closed. The dust on the cooker bore testimony to that fact.

Presently Cynth arrived and he watched through the open door as she went along the hall and into her room. He kept vigil, and twenty minutes later her door opened and she went to the bathroom along the corridor. He slipped out, along the corridor, and went inside. He could scarcely believe he was actually in her room. The seat of the beloved.

Forcing back dark thoughts of her copulating ferociously with Damien in this very room, he looked for somewhere to hide. There was only the wardrobe, which was more a large box than a proper piece of furniture. He got inside and among her clothes – blouses, skirts, a sweatshirt with the word GAS on it, knickers and some large bras. It was sort of kinky, but hardly the glorious entry to her inner sanctum he had imagined; he was a sneak rather than a conquering hero. But what was it Frank Finch had said? Love has to have a strategy too. This was love and war. He would wait and … what?

Now he was here he wasn't exactly sure what he would do. If Damien arrived he would leap from the wardrobe and denounce him – tell the beloved that Damien had tried it on with Helen. Somehow that didn't sound much now, especially as he'd been rejected. Having a wank on the desk wasn't too attractive, but maybe she wouldn't mind that either. To judge from her own behaviour, her views must be pretty liberal, and anyway Damien would probably say he'd been thinking of her and was overcome with passion. He'd called her a fat bitch but he'd just deny that.

Nothing for it, he'd have to lie. He'd say … and then it struck him. The full realisation. If he hadn't been crammed into a box masquerading as a wardrobe, almost stifled by the clothes of his beloved, he would have hit himself. Why hadn't he made the connection before?

He'd read some of her poems. They were staggeringly good. She was a class act. It vindicated his judgement. He had known she had depth, and he had been proven right. He especially liked two poems, called 'Watching You Leave' and 'Cloud Messages' and what had he seen on Damien's desk? A congratulatory note to Damien, mentioning those two poems as if he had been the writer. He'd apparently even got a bloody job in America on the basis of it, and a book was being published.

Damien the plagiarist. It would be so sweet to expose that rutting sod, especially if he came to see Cynth now. She might even kill him and she and Trevor could consummate their love over his hideous corpse. It would be macabre, and probably illegal, but darkly romantic.

The door opened and Cynth came in. She looked around furtively and Trevor's heart beat wildly as he thought she knew he was there and his courage and glee from a moment before shrivelled. She reached under her bed and took out a tin with a picture of a building on it. A cathedral or something, Trevor thought. She opened it and took out a Twix bar, then thought better and put it back. She opened a can of Dr Pepper and took a swig, then turned away from him and started to fiddle with something on her bedside cabinet. Then she turned back and started to eat sweets from her hand. She obviously had the munchies. She took another drink of Dr Pepper. What was it he'd read before he fell in love and lost his concentration: "There is no excellent beauty that hath not some strangeness in the proportion."

It was nice, sitting here, cocooned in Cynth's underwear, watching her eat sweets. Intimate. Almost domestic. He would remember this moment when … except he realised, with a lurch of bile in his stomach, that they weren't sweets at all. They were bloody pills, and she'd taken about sixty of them!

Trevor leapt from the wardrobe, but his foot caught in a bra and the whole thing fell on top of him. He struggled to his feet, gesticulating like a mad scarecrow, with knickers and t-shirts twirling like bunting all over him. Cynth turned and opened her mouth in amazement. Trevor lunged at her, missed and fell flat on his face. She stared at him, unfrightened, somehow far away from what was happening around her. Trevor struggled to his feet.

"Wait! You can't do this! What about the Yorkshire terriers and the Renault? Jesus Christ, we haven't even done it yet! You're too young to die. I mean, I know it's romantic and everything, but you can sort of imagine it without actually doing it. You wait here – I'll get a doctor. Don't move. Lie down."

He ran from the room, and then ran back again a moment later.

"No, don't lie down. You have to keep moving. Walk around. Come on, get up. I thought your poems were bloody fantastic! Get up. Come on!"

He helped her to her feet and tried to make her take a few steps. Then he saw her mobile phone on the bedside cabinet. He left her and grabbed it, then turned back to see her go very pale and fall heavily against the bed, cracking her head as she did so.

"Oh Jesus, oh bloody Shakespeare! Don't die! Don't die!"

He looked at the emergency numbers on the wall by the bed and dialled Dr Duff. The good doctor took a while to answer, as he was in the middle of a fiercely attritional tiebreak in the second set. The match could go either way. Unfortunately he lost so was not in the best of moods when he eventually answered.

"What is it? Do you have any idea of the time?" he snapped.

"Doctor, it's Cynth. She's …"

"Wait a minute," interrupted Dr Duff, as his opponent asked him if he'd like to go for a drink. He declined, partly because he'd lost, but also because the bar would be full of infected people and the glasses, unless washed and sterilised at least three times, would doubtless harbour all manner of disease-carrying bacteria. Eventually he got back to Trevor.

"Yes, now you were saying?"

"I was here already and sort of hiding in her room then she came back from the bathroom and …"

"Hiding in whose room?"

"Hers. Cynth's."

"And where were you hiding exactly?"

"In the wardrobe."

"A great mistake, young man. Are you aware that clothes harbour the dead cells of the body, flakes which are little galaxies of decay, dermatological holocausts?"

"But it's not me that needs help!"

"That's a matter of opinion. Who's the doctor here?"

"You are. But ..."

"Then but me no buts. I suggest you immediately have a shower, having cleaned it thoroughly beforehand, especially the nozzle. A scouring detergent is best. Then douse your whole body with a blend of tea tree oil and aloe vera, paying particular attention to those orifices prone to infection."

"Doctor, I'm trying to tell you about an emergency! Cynth is the girl I love and she's on the floor unconscious," sobbed Trev, sweat pouring down his face. Cynth had gone a terrible greenish colour.

"Don't I know your voice?" asked Dr Duff.

"Yes. I'm Trevor Bottom. I came to see you about sex."

"And now look where it's got you, Mr Bottom," said Dr Duff. "In a wardrobe full of scabrous body cells and a young woman unconscious in front of you. Didn't I warn you that sex was dangerous? The horror, the horror."

"We haven't even done it!"

"Then thank your lucky stars and get out of there while you still can."

Trevor hung up and rang 999. An automated voice gave him six options, but by the fifth he couldn't remember what the first four were. He stopped the call and dialled again, pressing any number once the automated voice started. He got a recording and left a garbled message saying he needed an ambulance very quickly.

Then he tried to get Cynth up and walking, but she collapsed. He sat on the floor with her, stroking her hair, her damp forehead, and worried about the significance of the various colour changes her face was undergoing. After what seemed like hours he looked out of the window. Then he saw two uniformed men jump out of an ambulance. One was eating a curry with a plastic spoon.

Trevor opened the door and gaped. The two men were horribly familiar.

"You're the security guards who ... who ..."

"Look who it ain't, Dave. The Professor hisself. Didn't recognise you with your clothes on," said Baz, belching and patting his stomach. "Think we can live on what they pay us, do you? Some bleedin' hopes. In the struggle for survival in the metropolitan jungle some rich arseholes call society, we poor bastards are forced to take on several jobs and work ourselves down to the bone. Take Dave here. Security, ambulance driver and pilates instructor."

Dave put down a silver foil carton containing the remnants of a chicken vindaloo.

"What you bin up to, then, pervy? S&M? Drugs, is it?" Dave asked.

"No, it's Cynth. She took an overdose. Please do something!"

They arranged their stretcher and Dave checked Cynth for a pulse and heartbeat.

"Course, what you got to worry about in these cases is brain damage. Now, if it'd been you there'd be no problem there, eh Prof?" said Baz cheerfully.

Dave chuckled.

With difficulty, they hefted Cynth onto the stretcher. Trevor provided reinforcements and, just as he bent down to cradle her head, she twitched slightly and threw up violently all over his chest. Then she fell back, unconscious.

"Just what the doctor ordered, eh Dave?" said Baz.

"Too right, Baz. Best thing when you OD is an almighty upchuck. Looks like codeine to me; could have been nasty. Still, you never know, might be a lot more where that came from best not count your chickens."

Trev looked down at the colourful, chocolaty mess on his chest, peppered with codeine tablets as if it had a strange, snowy infection, and thought: Now we've really made contact. This is real.

Chapter Thirty-Three

It was the silence that woke Frank.

After taking three painkillers he had slept fitfully, his head on the desk, and dreamed of Hamlet, a young man estranged in his own world, wondering who and what he is. Alienated homoeroticism, Mercedes Blonk had once called it, though where she got the homoeroticism from was anybody's guess. Seeing his father's ghost had unhinged something in Hamlet. Of course, it was metaphorical, or so Frank had always thought, but now as the world around him changed so alarmingly, he was less sure.

Sometimes in his dreams Margaret would sigh and smile at him, or he would turn in a supermarket queue and catch a glimpse of her disappearing behind an aisle, or getting on a train in the distance. Unlike Hamlet's father, she wasn't demanding revenge, retribution, redress, but something gentler. Compassion perhaps. Or steadfastness. Keeping to his lights. Yes, something like that – keeping to his lights, *their* lights. Whatever it was, he was grateful for these glimpses of someone, something, that spoke to him. It was a relief for which he gave thanks, for life had become bitterly cold and he was often sick at heart.

While he slept, the pipes had maintained a somnolent funereal beat then, suddenly, this stopped and Frank awoke, and knew things had changed forever yet again. Something had gone. It was time to go home. He trudged along the corridor and stopped outside Brimley's door. He thought he heard something. A whimper, a pitiful cry. Something small and suffering.

It must be the pipes, Frank thought, and trudged wearily towards the lift. He was beaten. He knew that.

The next morning a window cleaner lowered his cradle and looked into Brimley's room. By then Brimley was inert, utterly dehydrated, his tongue cleaved to his upper palate, and barely conscious. An hour later he was in hospital in intensive care, his bed screened from view, on a drip and lucky to be alive. He'd had three enemas.

Fifty feet below him lay Roy Fish on a white table, not alive at all. It seemed an obvious case of suicide. A highly strung academic, prone to conspiracy theories, increasingly losing touch with a changing world that threatened to leave him behind, then one day it all became too much. His neck must have snapped on impact when he made his death leap from the car park into the bushes far below. Jeremy Pickles shook his head sadly as he confirmed these salient details to the police sergeant investigating.

"Terrible to say, but I wasn't completely surprised. We offered counselling support, extended leave, but dear Roy was a proud man …" He let the unfinished sentence hang significantly in the air.

The sergeant nodded sagely and left. Jeremy Pickles breathed a sigh of relief and rang the porters to tell them to clear out Fish's office and bring all correspondence to him.

Why did the stupid bastard have to top himself? It was so inconvenient, so messy. All right, he was a pain in the arse, but why make himself a bigger one by drawing all this bad publicity? Some people were so inconsiderate. Still, clause 25C in all current employment contracts, skilfully inserted by Pickles himself, meant that, at a stroke, Fish's wife lost all pension rights. Top yourself and you forfeit the lot. It made the desperate think twice.

But despite the pleasure of having saved the university a full pension, it didn't feel tidy. Fish was most definitely not the sort of man to commit suicide, but to go down alternative routes would involve thoughts Pickles was not prepared to entertain. Not unless the Chancellor forced him to, and who knew what the Chancellor might want?

And now, it seemed, the fat girl he sent to Spinelli had tried to top herself as well. What on earth had the little tin pot tyrant done to her, for God's sake? Another cover up called for. God, was there no end to the work?

And to top it all, bloody Brimley Trevalyan in hospital after a night of pagan depravity in his office. To judge from the window cleaner and police statements he'd been involved in some sort of weird initiation rite involving human waste and large amounts of alcohol. He'd never have thought it of him. Jeremy had him down as a nasty little careerist, willing to shaft his own grandmother to get on. People like that were so easy to control, but obviously a little bit of power had gone to his head.

Jeremy puffed out his cheeks, clenched his buttocks and anticipated he would have to flex other muscles here and slap Trevalyan down. Probably best to do it while he was in hospital, catch him with his pants down so to speak.

High up in the Tower of light, Adam Bittermouth sat in his chair and clung tightly to the two metal rings screwed firmly to his desk. He had them put there for moments of extreme anxiety, when he needed ballast, something to hold fast to. A smoked salmon sandwich and a glass of chilled Sancerre had been delivered an hour ago and were still in the dumb waiter. But he couldn't risk letting go of the rings just yet. He concentrated on his breathing and thought of eternal life in a sky without end.

It wasn't anything specific that had caused the attack, more a worrying series of small things that rippled throughout the university: the sound of ambulances; those few minutes when cameras 303 through to 306 in the multi storey car park had gone blank; the increase in sexual perversity. It was all such messy human activity. Perhaps he should bring the master plan forward. People were so dirty and such a liability that how could the Dark Invader fail to notice?

He looked up. Was it his imagination or had the ceiling lowered slightly? He imagined a catastrophically huge Rosemary Puddock rearing down on the Tower, her giant breasts swinging like wrecking balls to flatten his beautiful Tower. God, he should have built it higher. It should have reached the clouds. He would be safe there, hidden in Olympian floss.

He counted aloud to ten and took a few deep breaths. It's all right, it's all right, it's all right, he intoned like a mantra. Suddenly, the mood passed and he recovered. Then he knew – Pickles was keeping something from him. That's what had caused it. He rang through.

"Sir, I was just about to …" Pickles' voice said.

"No you weren't. You were keeping things from me," said Adam.

"No, no, Sir. It's nothing and I didn't want to worry you."

"Didn't want to worry me? Didn't want to worry me, you say. Pickles, I am extremely worried. I am worried that in about five minutes you will be out of a job and I'll have to find another poodle to train, that's what I'm worried about. Now tell me what's been happening."

"Fish committed suicide. A student also apparently tried to kill herself but didn't. So it's nothing serious."

"And our erstwhile Professor of Quality Assurance? What if the press gets hold of that? "

"I'm sorry. I'll attend to everything, Chancellor."

"Yes you will. I want more surveillance cameras, more security guards, and I want the Final Solution brought forward. By next year I want the student population halved and the academic staff down by seventy five per cent."

"That might be difficult, Chancellor …"

"Good! Because I want you to work very hard indeed. I want you to encounter enormous difficulties and suffer something like the stress I have been under because of you. And I want a raised roof on my Tower, on steel poles, one that will reflect light back so that anyone looking down will be blinded."

"But Sir, nobody could look down. They'd have to be five hundred feet tall. And we've already bribed, I mean *persuaded*, the airlines not to fly over."

"Pickles, what are you going to do the moment I hang up?"

Now the tone was quiet, snake-like. It was the tone Jeremy hated and feared most.

"I'm going to get a raised reflecting surface roof erected on the Tower of Light, then I'm going to see to everything else you mentioned."

The receiver clicked as the Chancellor switched off his hands-free. He had spoken. He had been heard.

But the problem was, Jeremy thought, now I've got to act, which is easier said than done. He wasn't at all sure the Tower of Light could stand the weight of a raised roof. It would had the original design specifications been implemented, but they had not. Nor had the university plumbing specifications.

Jeremy had met a builder, Kenny Robinson, at some forgettable fund-raising function and Kenny had said that if he got the contract, no questions asked, he could build the Tower and do all of Roebuck's plumbing for a million less than the original or any other estimate. That meant that with a bit of paper shifting, a little figure finessing, some graph manipulation, Jeremy Pickles would be a made man.

Health and safety and building regulations were just a matter of a few backhanders, which good old Kenny dealt with. For his efforts, Jeremy even arranged for Kenny to get an OBE for services to industry. And Jeremy got two offshore accounts worth a million pounds. He wouldn't touch them yet. That would be foolish. In years to come, however, whatever happened he was a millionaire.

It wasn't enough, though. He still wanted status, to be a public figure, to win the respect of the enigmatic Adam Bittermouth, and finally to be Chancellor himself. Money was great, but so was power and getting people to jump.

Chapter Thirty-Four

Trev went to the hospital with Cynth and sat in a cheerless waiting room in which the fluorescent lights buzzed like insects, the coffee machine didn't work and the only other people were a drunk who kept asking Trevor for money, a pugnacious looking boy of no more than fifteen with a black eye and a bleeding nose who kept muttering darkly "Oi'll fuckin' git 'im. Oi'll fuckin' git 'im," and a woman who had her head caught in a lampshade, so that it frilled around her neck like a freshly shampooed circus poodle.

Cynth had been rushed off for a brain scan and to have her stomach pumped out, although most of what had been there had now dried on Trevor's t-shirt and smelt distinctly high. Even the drunk moved away from him. A nice looking Asian nurse asked Trevor if he would like to borrow a hospital shirt and he blushed furiously and thanked her. When she brought it to him he wondered if it was difficult for a nurse to get excited about men when she'd seen so many of them, most of whom were ill, injured and extremely sorry for themselves. He wanted to ask if she'd ever shaved a man's privates but thought she might take it the wrong way.

He waited all night. Eventually, in the morning, a doctor arrived and asked if he was a relative.

"Not quite," he said, reddening to his roots. "I mean, we have an understanding, sort of. At least I do."

"Was this a lover's tiff then?" asked the doctor.

"No, no. I mean, she'd just been with this funny little mad bloke with a moustache and went back to her room. She might have been waiting for Damien. And I was there too. Hiding in the wardrobe. But …"

"All right," said the doctor, not wishing to hear any more. It had been a long night. "Would you like to see her?"

"Yes," said Trevor.

She was asleep and he thought: If this was a fairy tale I'd kiss her, she'd awaken and we'd live happily ever after. Recent experience had taught him that reality was much more irksome, unruly and predictable. He would like to ask Dr Finch if it was best to behave as if life was predictable, and to plan regardless of what actually happened, or to sit back and just let the storm of reality play over you and hope you are still alive when it passes.

He held Cynth's hand and the warmth of her body seeped into him. He felt tired to his bones and a few minutes later his head slowly dipped and cradled into Cynth's peacefully heaving bosom.

He was roused a few hours later by furious whispering from the next bed. He couldn't see who was there because there was a screen separating the two areas, but it was obviously getting very nasty. He listened.

"But Jeremy, I nearly died in that room!"

"Nearly, nearly. Poor baby. The fact is you're still here, and still employed by the university for the time being. The Chancellor is furious with you." Jeremy Pickles' words were indistinct as he ate the grapes he'd bought for Brimley.

"Did he … did he say that?" asked Brimley miserably.

"Yes. And he also said that he wants you to implement a decisive cull. Ten members of staff by Christmas, and now the digital course packages are taking off we can shed students, too. English loses forty percent this year and no new intake."

"You mean just chuck them out?"

"Yes. We'll blame the government. Fees too high. We can't cope. Nobody will care. In a few years time, when we're rid of all students and most staff, Roebuck will be at the top of the digital and distance learning pile anyway and others will follow suit. It's not about education, it's about good business practice – we both know that."

He leaned back, relaxing slightly for the first time that day and even forgetting to whom he was talking. "You know, what people don't realise is that knowledge is redundant. Power and profit lie in the provision of information and all you have to do is make information masquerade as knowledge. One day people will, quite literally, know nothing and think they know everything. But even as Registrar I can't do it all myself, so the sooner you get your arse out of here and back to Roebuck, the sooner you don't lose your job."

Mention of his posterior reminded Brimley of his recent nightmare, and of the frightening volume of padding, rubber and tubing around his frail body. His wife had been to see him and had seemed strangely unsympathetic. Women had no imagination. They can only see things from their limited point of view, he thought miserably.

"Another thing," said Pickles. "I almost forgot. A girl in your department tried to kill herself. Overdose. She's all right, but I don't want bad publicity. Take an interest. Write to her family. Her name's … Christ, I can't remember. Something … Fat girl"

Trevor mouthed the blessed name: Cynth.

"But I don't know any of the students. I mean – I'm not there to teach or anything. I'm there to …"

"Precisely. So get on with it. Especially as you clearly aren't going to finish your book on Ronald Drain."

"Why not? It was progressing very well and …"

"He wrote a piece about you in the Independent this morning. What was it? Ah, yes: 'My would-be biographer reminded me of something I once found blocking my toilet – inert, useless and obliviously free of thought or feeling.' I think the book is definitely off." Pickles chuckled for the first time in many days.

The Registrar left, taking the remaining grapes with him, and Brimley sank back wearily. He shifted his weight and, despite the morphine and soothing ointments, everywhere seemed impossibly sore. He would be sore for months, the doctor happily said. He lay on a rubber ring that squeaked obscenely every time he moved. People would laugh at him.

Less than two yards away Trevor was processing a great deal of information and wondering what to make of it all. All sorts of plans were forming, dissembling and reforming. His fingers itched to make a list.

Chapter Thirty-Five

It was cold. The crematorium was a cheerless place and, as he drove up to it, Frank smelt a faint choke in the air. Something burning, something gone. Smoke and ashes.

Now in a cold, large room he stood next to Jane Fish, her two sons either side, uncannily resembling their father with the sloping forehead and glitteringly intelligent eyes. Outside the flowers were incongruous against grey stone and a metal grille: roses from the family, sweet pea and rhododendrons from Frank (and Margaret – he couldn't help himself and wrote her name) and some daisies from the Registry bearing a £10.50 sticker. The Chancellor had sent a little replica of the Tower of Light.

Fish had little patience with God, whom he had considered to be both inefficient if he had existed, and a waste of time thinking about because he didn't; so this was a secular affair and Jane had asked Frank to say a few words to the assembled. He had wanted to tell her that he would have to decline because he was in the process of becoming barking mad, but just as he'd picked up the telephone in his office the pipes suddenly sounded a chorus of *Alleluia! Alleluia!* and he knew that, even if he made a hash of it, he couldn't refuse the wife of an old comrade in arms.

He'd taken six painkillers and it was only ten in the morning. Everything looked glassy and opaque. He stood and shuffled onto a little podium near the oak and walnut coffin with shiny brass handles. Roy would have smiled at this, and found some clever way of placing it without losing reverence for the dead. He began.

"Death is not an eccentricity, but a settled habit of the universe, and a man's dying is more the survivors' affair than his own. So we are here to grieve, and to celebrate Roy's life. The time of life is short; to spend that shortness basely were too long. Roy Fish, my friend and colleague, did no such thing. He had more integrity than anyone I can recall. Master of himself, frighteningly clever, unwavering in his ability to condemn the fault and the actor of it.

"George Bernard Shaw said that liberty means responsibility, and that is why most men dread it. Roy didn't. He accepted it, no matter whom it offended. He hated the abuse of power and even at the end he ..." And he caught someone moving, looking at him. It was Jeremy Pickles. He could see ... but he didn't want to see and turned to look at the clock at the back of the room. Ten past ten. "Even at the end ..." Was that Margaret at the back of the hall? Dear Margaret, smiling? He was aware he was faltering. Jane looked at him and nodded. He took strength from it, but could also see ... he looked away.

"Roy flinched at nothing. He knew that life is a perpetual dying. He believed in eternal verities – justice, truth – and was ever willing to bid goodbye to anything or anyone who stood in their way. This is courage indeed. The drums of today call to us, as they called to young Fortinbras in Hamlet. We praise the pioneer, but let us not praise him on wrong grounds. His strength lies not in his leaning out to new things – that may be mere curiosity – but in his power to abandon old things. All his courage is a courage of adieus. Roy reminded us of this ..."

He looked up and his breath caught. Who was that in the corner in a bright blue dress, smiling, blonde, knowing? A memory stirred, but not his own, or was it? Could memories belong to someone else? She blew him a kiss. And there, just in front of her, a sad young man with dark curls and holding a sword. Who the hell was he? And even as he knew, he recoiled from the thought.

Jane was looking at him again and this time he couldn't look away. Take a full look at the worst. After all, it was only telling him what he already knew. She was thinking of Roy alive, articulate, sometimes mocking and Puckish, but ferociously honourable and with that image words circled like smoke around it: *"He did not kill himself. My husband did not kill himself. He would not do that to me."*

She was right. Of course she was right. Frank drew a deep breath and changed course. He took a crumpled letter from his pocket.

"I received this from Roy a few days ago. He objected to a tyrant being given a place to study at Roebuck merely because he is rich. Quite rightly, Roy was outraged by this, but was the only person who knew about it to have the courage to make a stand."

He paused and saw the weight of his words hang on all present. Jane's eyes shone with tears, but they were proud tears. Frank could feel the eyes of Jeremy Pickles trying to bore a hole through his heart. He looked at him, but this time did not flinch, and what he saw made him know he was doing the right thing. There, in the eyes and behind them, a sort of twitching brick wall that kept crumbling and re-forming, crumbling and re-forming. Frank was a literary bloke. He knew about metaphors. He had a pretty good idea what was behind that wall. It wasn't guilt. You needed a conscience, a moral sensibility for that. It was doubt. This was a man trying to hide something, probably as much from himself as from anyone else. He took another letter from his pocket and cleared his throat.

"This is from my illustrious Professor Brimley Trevalyan. *'Dear Dr Finch, it has come to my attention that you have received a letter from Dr Roy Fish regarding the PhD student Vittorio Spinelli. The letter is a scurrilous attack on the student. Further, there are procedures for making complaints, and private correspondence is not part of that process.*

"'Dr Fish is an ambitious man, and may have his own agenda. In any case, the Registrar and I have no doubt you will disregard the contents, especially as they may involve you in litigation. The worst-case scenario is dismissal for bringing the university into disrepute.

"Yours etc, Professor Brimley Trevalyan.'"

All eyes were on Frank. He continued: "The good Professor tells us that Roy was ambitious to a fault. He was my friend, but Professor Trevalyan tells us he was ambitious, and Trevalyan is an honourable man. Roy brought great honour to the university with intelligent books and research grants, but Trevaylan tells us he was ambitious, with his own agenda, and Trevalyan is an honourable man.

"Students respected Roy, and twice he refused a Pro Vice-Chancellorship because he was more interested in ideas than administration, but Trevaylan says he was ambitious and Trevaylan is an honourable man.

"Roy was known nationally and internationally for sniffing out corruption and often fighting on behalf of the underdog, but Trevalyan and the Registrar say he was ambitious, with his own agenda, and they are honourable men.

"You may ask how Trevalyan and the Registrar knew the contents of Roy's private correspondence, but they are honourable men. I say only what I know. Roy, we are told, took his own life. The Registrar and the Chancellor believe that, no doubt, and they are honourable men. "

He stopped and looked up to see Jeremy Pickles leaving the crematorium, a butcher's smile on his face. The woman in the blue dress smiled saucily at him and winked. The young man with the sword nodded. There were others, new people, approving presences, including a strange, gloomy figure sitting hunched and alone, muttering to himself, but Frank had taken off his glasses and they were too shadowy to discern. Never mind, they'll be back, he thought, and he stepped down, suddenly weary, feeling very old, but unburdened.

He was finished at Roebuck, but it didn't matter. He would go back there anyway. He quite wanted to see how that mad young lover was getting on. He wanted his books around him. He was surprised at how lucid he'd been. It felt like a swan song.

As he left the crematorium, he was aware of a fracas going on behind him. Roy's two sons and his widow were physically restraining officials from drawing the curtain and incinerating the corpse. Jane was clinging to the coffin as if it was a surfboard keeping her afloat. There would be another, more rigorous autopsy. Nobody was having Roy's body until it had told its story, revealed its truth.

Frank chuckled. Even in death Roy was a fighter, hounding his enemies from beyond the grave.

Chapter Thirty-Six

Cynth was still asleep. Trevor was about to go back to the university for a quick shower and change of clothes, then return, when he heard a familiar voice from behind the curtain.

"Just popped in to say Ciao," said Damien.

Trevor fought back the urge to go through and tell the hated Damien that he knew all about the poems, and to hit him around the head with the fire extinguisher, but he decided to hear what he had to say first.

"Never had you down as a sex games freako, but whatever turns you on," said Damien.

"Is there some point to this visit, Damien, given that you've just ensured you won't set foot on Roebuck campus ever again, except to clear out your office?" said Brimley, shifting his weight uncomfortably, and aware that the menace of his tone was somewhat undermined by the squelching of the rubber ring he was squirming on.

"Nice one. It's the Michelin man. Yeh, I'm off to the land of wine and sunshine. Sweet California. Professor of Poetry and Creative Writing at the University of Southern California. And Penguin is rushing out my latest collection. Shame, Roebuck could have kept me. Frankly, I don't think you could afford me now."

Damien took a bottle of champagne from a carrier bag and popped the cork, which flew over the curtain and landed with a plop on Cynth's slowly rising and falling bosom. Trevor picked it up. He knew exactly the place for that cork as he heard Damien slurp champagne.

"If, by some extraordinary error of judgement, any of this is true, then I can only say that the most pleasant thing about it will be your absence," said Brimley.

"It's cool then. Well, can't stand around exchanging

pleasantries all day. Visas to get, clothes to buy, shades to try on. Ciao," said Damien, and minced away.

Trevor had to restrain himself. Revenge is indeed a dish best served cold. He wanted to savour it. He turned the cork around in his hand, very slowly. The champagne bottle had also given him an idea. He was still thinking about the detail when Cynth yawned and woke up. She blinked and looked at Trevor.

"Hi," he said.

She stared at him, then at the tubes in her arm, the ward. It was all so confusing.

"You tried to kill yourself but, luckily, I was hiding in your wardrobe and called an ambulance. How are you feeling?"

She shrugged.

"Yes. Probably take a while. Don't talk if you're too tired. I'll just sort of ramble on a bit, shall I? Or I could shut up. Funny how you babble when you're nervous.

"I had an uncle who went off his chump and he used to talk all the time to these voices only he could hear who told him to do terrible things. Anyway they got so fed up with him – the doctors and nurses, not the voices – that they gave him a lobotomy, you know, where they cut off a bit of your brain at the front. And when they took off the bandages he started walking around the hospital shouting even louder than before: 'Speak up, you buggers, I can't hear you any more but I know you're there.'

"Hey, I don't want you to think it runs in the family or anything. I mean, I'm just normal and ..." Trevor started to blush, but an amazing thing had happened.

Cynth was smiling. It was a real heartfelt smile. It only lasted a moment but it was the best thing that had happened to Trevor since he found out he'd got a place at university. And she didn't seem to be smiling at him and thinking what an uncool nerd he was; she was smiling *with* him. They were together. He was about to propose marriage, but she suddenly seemed sleepy and her eyes started to droop again.

The nice Asian nurse who may or may not have shaved a man's privates came and insisted that Trevor leave for a while. He could come back at evening visiting time. Cynth needed to rest.

An hour later he was in his room, his whole life transformed by her smile. He could do anything now. She'd smiled at him. She'd been glad he was there. The fact that she'd instantly fallen asleep made him anxious that the interest hadn't lasted long, but she had tried to kill herself and taken an overdose not long before, so there probably wasn't anything to really worry about. He felt full of resolve as he tore down all the useless lists and bundled them into bin liners.

When full, he dragged them out to the back of his hall and along the grass to where flowed a turgid little stream, referred to on the campus map as Bittermouth Springs. Near the stream he emptied out all the lists, took some book matches from his pocket and lit them.

He watched as the thousands of words and numbers, the metre upon metre of tortured hierarchies browned and crisped and ignited and finally smoked their madness into the October air.

All that frenetic energy, the agonising attempt to order the world, when he now realized that the more you tried to order and control things, the more they rebelled. All you could do was face things square on as they happened. You could still act and let the world know you're there – he certainly intended to do that – but you had to accept that the consequences would probably be other than you imagined. Now he had realized this, he felt a delirious sense of freedom and laughed to himself.

He felt in his pocket and took out the champagne cork. He again heard the 'pop' it had made as it shot from the bottle, but it was louder, more explosive, this time. That, plus watching his lists transform into flames and smoke gave him a clearer idea of what he must do. It was like the *Aeneid*. Fate. Caprice. His newfound strength came from a sense that it didn't matter what drove events. One explanation was as good, and as false, as another.

From his elevated sanctuary Adam watched the fire consuming the lists via a mini camera secreted in a treetop. He was finding this morning particularly nerve-wracking because work had begun on his new roof and the thought that there were people both near and higher than him was distressing. Nevertheless he steeled his nerves and zoomed in on the burning lists: kiss; war; desire; fight; lips; victory. It all sounded very anarchic and unruly. Was the strange looking student grinning to himself destroying pornography? University files?

He was just about to call security when something more alarming caught his eye. On another monitor he saw Frank Finch walking mournfully to his room. Of course, Jeremy Pickles had informed Adam of what had happened at the funeral, because since Adam had put a rocket under him he was frightened of concealing anything, though he still had an uneasy sense there were things he didn't know. What could they be? For now, it was insupportable that Finch should be allowed back on the campus. He'd betrayed them all.

Adam would like to see him imprisoned. Why not? The man is an informer, an outsider; he has committed apostasy and should be punished. He may even have collaborated with the Dark Invader. He switched on the monitor in Jeremy Pickles' room but was so astonished at what he saw that all thoughts of Frank Finch dissolved.

Pickles was being held spread-eagled over his own desk by two large and identical men and General Spinelli was holding a large, vicious looking curved knife against his Registrar's groin. The look on the little General's shiny face suggested he had every intention of using the knife. Pickles was a fool. What had he done to incur such wrath? What crashing goof had he made this time? Until recently Adam had trusted Pickles, the way a snake trusts a mouse not to harm him. Now he was beginning to have second thoughts. Once these current blips were sorted out satisfactorily he would have to look around for a new oberlieutenant. The Final Solution couldn't be jeopardized by one man's reckless incompetence.

Jeremy Pickles was indeed in fear of, if not his life, at least that part of his life that involved relieving himself and possible procreation, had he been interested in women, which he certainly was not. The General had burst into his room with Boris and Boris and asked why Cynth had not come to his apartment. He assumed that Pickles should have taken personal responsibility for both discovering and ensuring the fulfillment of his wishes.

Pickles then made the supreme mistake of not taking the General seriously and said that, given that Cynth was a student, perhaps she had work to do, and anyway it wasn't his responsibility to track the lives of every student – he had more important things to do. In a flash Boris and Boris held him down and the General had taken out his knife.

Boris and Boris had been through the student files, having knocked unconscious a secretary who complained, and found Cynth's room number. However she was not there. Prone to paranoia, the General immediately assumed that someone was keeping her from him and went straight to the Registrar.

Pickles' arrogant tone, induced by his indignation at the funeral of that bastard Fish, had been a mistake of the first order, as he was now discovering. Spinelli was a man who believed in the direct route.

"I iss cuttings off your cajones iffen you not finding thees one wimmins Cynth. Beleefings me, I do not beat up the bush. You findings out now, Peekles! I come back in thees one 'our and you telling me then, or ..." He made an unmistakable and well practised gesture with the knife, his breath smelling of tobacco plantations and garlic oil.

He let Pickles go and the terrified Registrar immediately got through to his secretary on the intercom to discover the whereabouts of Cynth. If she were still in hospital it wouldn't take long. He'd have to throw her to the wolves to save himself and deal with damage limitation afterwards.

Chapter Thirty-Seven

Trev sat at a long desk on the science floor of the library, his laptop open and humming quietly, and pondered.

The world had cracked open. The possibilities that now poured through the gap made him feel light headed. Cynth had smiled at him. He'd saved her life. He'd actually saved her life! That was bloody heroic. That was the *Aeneid* and Homer and Shakespeare and all of them rolled into one. It would make a fantastically racy chapter in his semi-autobiographical novel, now provisionally entitled either *Life of a Romantic Anarchist* or *Confessions of a Campus Warrior*. David Bowie said we could be heroes just for one day and Trevor felt his day was fast approaching. He'd saved the girl he loved, and now he would do something equally dramatic. That's what heroes did – they did something dramatic then they either died or got the girl.

The idea of what he should do was like crystals in his mind that kept forming and breaking down, then re-forming. It had something to do with the champagne cork and retribution, specifically against Damien, but that could wait, and against that little mad-looking bloke, but that could wait too. After years of tortured self-preoccupation Trevor Bottom now looked out and saw the bigger picture and it offended him deeply.

He had heard the Registrar and Professor Trevalyan talk contemptuously about students – about him and Cynth. After working like buggery to get to university and acquiring a whopping debt for his student loan, he now discovered that the people who ran it were a bunch of sniping little shits who didn't give a toss about someone like him.

And there was the further question of the children he and Cynth would have. They'd have no chance at all of getting into university if the likes of Professor Trevalyan and the Registrar were running things; and he suspected that it was nearly always the case that their ilk did run things. They were going to stop his children from having a decent education. How dare they?

And the Registrar called Cynth a fat girl. He didn't even know her name. And he'd ridiculed knowledge, something his mad visionary friend – as he now considered him – Dr Finch would never do. Perhaps Finch was the only decent faculty member left, and he was bonkers. This led Trevor to conclude that one needed a little madness, a little recklessness, a little daring.

He restored the laptop page he'd been looking at. It was astonishing that you could find things like this on the Internet. Even a few days ago, he would have been outraged, but now he just felt the hard glitter of knowing how the world wagged. It all looked astonishingly easy. Household goods, off-the-shelf things, get the weights and measurements right, and you've got an effective bomb. No wonder there were so many terrorists if it was so easy. He took the champagne cork from his pocket and the sound it had made now registered even louder in his memory. Like an explosion. He threw it in the air, caught it, and smiled.

He found 638,812 websites that helped the would-be bomber. He discovered there were books, journals and magazines like *The Anarchist's Cookbook, Household Bomb Recipes, Ruining People's Lives with Small Explosions, The Householder's Guide to the A Bomb*, and *Have Fun with a Bedside Stun Gun*. In an article entitled *The Home Owner's Guide to Making a Nuclear Bomb*, it was patiently explained that people had got it all wrong about radiation:

> *Myth: Radiation is bad for you.*
> *Fact: Everything is bad for you if you have too much of it.*
> *Eat too many bananas and you'll get a stomach ache. If you get too much sun you'll get burned or even develop skin cancer. Same thing with radiation. Too much may make*

you feel under the weather, but nuclear officials insist that low-level radiation has no really serious adverse effects. And high-level radiation may bring unexpected benefits. It speeds up evolution by weeding out unwanted genetic types and creating new ones. (Remember the old saying, "Two heads are better than one.") Nearer to home, it's plain that radiation will get rid of pesky crab grass and weeds, and teenagers will find that brief exposure to a nuclear burst vaporizes acne and other skin blemishes.

It also then said, somewhat tangentially, that it was a known fact that most vegetarians are impotent and that solar energy is a communist conspiracy. Among these assertions, which Trevor strongly suspected had little scientific basis, were practical instructions for making explosive devices. He was about to copy the instructions to a disk when he heard a snigger and looked around.

Boris and Boris were sitting on a couple of easy chairs just behind him, smoking Bulgarian cigarettes and drinking schnapps. A librarian was giving them dirty looks from behind his desk, but they ignored him and he lacked the courage to actually confront them. They looked as if they might casually dismember him as a spider would a fly.

They came into the library every day for a happy hour of drinking and smoking. What prompted the snigger was when Boris saw what was on Trevor's laptop, and he nudged Boris in the ribs to look at it too.

"What's the joke?" said the newly fearless Trevor.

"That is," said Boris.

"No good," said Boris.

"Right, and I s'pose you know all about making explosives," scoffed Trevor.

Boris and Boris looked at each other. This spotty youth seemed to have no fear of them. It made them warm to him. They were so used to meeting spineless apparatchiks on this windy campus that he was refreshing.

"Yes," said Boris.

"Ve do," said Boris.

"So what's wrong with it?" asked Trevor.

"No salt," said Boris.

"Salt no good," said Boris.

They explained that baking powder was what he needed, or: "A little fertilizer, some bleach and some hubcaps to put them all in, and you heff a bomb," Boris said.

"You can use frozen orange juice and slugs if you got none bleach," Boris added helpfully.

Trevor turned his chair around. These guys were interesting. In the next half hour he learned an amazing amount and he reasoned that this was precisely what university was meant for: the acquisition of knowledge. He learned there were: Co2 canister bombs, aerosol bombs, lightbulb bombs, pipe bombs, rocket powder mixture bombs, baking soda bombs, acetone bombs, more acetone bombs, acid bombs, bleach explosives, book bombs, AFPO explosive cattle prods, ammonium tri-iodide crystals, astrolite and sodium chlorate bottle bombs, another bottle bomb, bulls-eye explosive, cherry bombs, chlorine gas bombs, Coke can bombs, milk carton bombs. Also of interest were things like vomit gas, black powder chlorates and perclorates.

At the end, his head was reeling with the poetry of destruction. Boris and Boris enjoyed blowing off a little steam with this strangely unfrightened young man. He clearly had a hunger to learn and thanked them for the information.

Then Boris got a call on his mobile. "Ve heff now to go to hospital," he said.

Trevor looked at his watch. "Me too," he said. "Which one?"

"St Leonard's," said Boris.

"That's weird. I'm going there," said Trevor, thinking that he was fated to meet these two kindred anarchist spirits.

"Then ve giff you lift. Our boss he don't mind. He like people to talk to," said Boris.

Ten minutes later, Trevor was sitting in the back of a Lincoln Continental. The interior was so big you could play skittles should you feel the urge. There was a TV and a bar and telephones. He sat back and thought how strange his first term had been. Then the door opened and General Spinelli got in. Trevor blanched. The General smiled.

"So, you iss fellow student? Good. I am one PhD radical transerlationist. I go to this hospital to seeing my girlfriend. Soon we iss being married. My sixth wifes. My ham being like your king 'Enry – Yes? The other wifes no good. No importa. They die tragicerally. This one different. She – 'ow you say – one 'ell of a wimmins."

Trevor looked blank. This could be the ride back to hell.

Chapter Thirty-Eight

Frank sat at his desk, weary to the bones. "How long now?" he asked no one in particular.

"Not long," the answer came, and he looked around.

For a second, in the corner, a smile and a toss of a blonde curl, then the pipes clicked on and Vaughan Williams' *Lark Ascending* began. It was almost more than he could bear just now. *Lark Ascending* was the music he and Margaret had chosen that crisp winter morning when their dog Jemma had died.

At the surgery, on a table in a little consulting room, she had looked at him trustingly while the nurse shaved a patch on her front leg. A tiny speck of blood formed, then the vet injected her, all the while Frank stroking her and telling her how beautiful she was and what adventures they'd had. Telling her that everything was all right, that she was a good girl. Her head dipped to the right and her eyes closed, then she recovered momentarily, looked up, dipped again, her eyes flickered and she slumped to the right. The vet caught her. Frank held her and was overwhelmed with the finality of it all.

She went to her death quietly because she trusted him implicitly, and he couldn't help feeling his one last act with her was one of betrayal, a Judas kiss.

"She's gone," the vet said.

Frank held her and kissed her head. She gave a violent paroxysm.

"That's normal," said the vet.

Jemma exhaled loudly, and Frank was reminded of the many things he'd read about death, the soul leaving with the last breath.

He went home feeling an ache that clamped his heart shut, sat watching the cold, too bright morning outside, then made up his mind and went back to the vet's surgery. He brought her home shrouded in a white sheet, then dug a deep hole in the garden by the shed, beneath the holly tree. He placed her gently inside, facing the house, a few precious things for her journey: a well-chewed miniature rugby ball; her collar with name and engraved address; her favourite toy, a coloured plastic walking stick; a photograph of the four of them (David smiling and holding Jemma tightly, her head leaning up and trying to kiss his giggling face). He and Margaret stood there for a while, both tearful then, as they left, a flock of Canada geese flew overhead, all golden in the morning sun, honking the *Last Post*.

"That's for Jemma," said Margaret.

Indoors was coffee and *Lark Ascending* with its rising and falling cadences, its little trills of hope and mourning and newness.

And suddenly, now an old man alone in his office, Frank was there again, his head in his hands, sobbing like a child for everything that had left him but still gnawed at his heart. He wouldn't swap the pain for all the gold in the world. It made it all real. Nevertheless he swallowed two painkillers to ease his throbbing head and a deep ache in his left side.

Along the corridor Damien took a last look around his room. He hadn't bothered to tidy it. Leaving it in a complete mess, strewn with coffee cups, wine bottles and piles of paper was a bit Bohemian, a bit rock 'n' roll. Really, he should trash the place just for the hell of it, but he had a date, then a plane to catch. California. Fame. Mega bucks. The whole fucking caboodle.

It had been difficult, the decision to leave his wife, but it just wouldn't have worked. She wouldn't have fitted in, and part of his job as a poet, he now felt with increasing clarity and conviction, was to look uncomfortable truths in the face. Emotional and intellectual honesty. His marriage was over. He'd tried to explain this gently to her but it had all become acrimonious and the scene didn't have the tragic clarity he'd envisaged. She called him a talentless, selfish wanker. She was upset, she didn't mean it, of course, but nevertheless he felt a little wounded. It all seemed unnecessarily messy and, as he walked out of the door, he said he'd send money. His son could visit once he was settled, once things were OK. Once his shit was together.

He decided he probably wouldn't marry again. There were too many attendant problems, too many compromises, and it cramped his spontaneity. Part of becoming mature was to recognise what sort of animal you really were, and Damien now knew he was a free spirit. That was his destiny. And he would be leaving with a satisfying bang.

He'd met Heidi, the PhD student with big tits, in the lift the day before and invited her to his room today. Before getting out of the lift, he'd given her a kiss and she'd responded favourably. (He had to dispel the memory of Cynth in the same lift.) Now it was Wednesday afternoon at Roebuck, study time, which meant no classes and, therefore, no interruptions from bloody students. He opened his last bottle of white wine.

Then there was a knock at the door. He was looking forward to this. He had an idea – it would be hilarious, and sexy, and she'd love it. A minute later the door opened and Damien jumped from behind it, bollock naked, his hands outstretched in an extravagant showbiz welcome.

"Da da!"

Baz and Dave stood there for a moment then, with a surprising agility, Dave was onto Damien and had him in a painful arm lock on the floor.

"Shall I break 'is bleeding arm, Baz? I meanterfuckinsay, perv's askin' for it. Makes me sick. Taxpayer's money," said Dave.

"Nah," said Baz thoughtfully. "Break 'is leg instead. That should pedestrianise his overarching ambitions for a while."

"Make the bleeder think twice too, I should say," said Dave, changing the hold to Damien's leg and applying a pressure that made Damien dizzy with pain.

"Please, it's all a mistake. You don't understand. I'm a poet. I'm going to America," he squealed, and tears sprung to his eyes.

"Hospital's where you're going first, Sunshine," said Dave, twisting his leg a little more.

Then Baz got a call on his mobile. He listened and his face registered a profound disappointment.

"Right, Guv'nor," said Baz and stopped the call. "Let 'im go, Dave."

Dave's jaw dropped. He looked like a little boy whose favourite toy had just been snatched from him.

"Why's that. Baz?"

"'Im upstairs," said Baz, raising his eyes, a gesture which always indicated the Chancellor at Roebuck.

"Oh. Right. 'Owd 'e know?"

"'E works in mysterious ways," said Baz.

They left just as Heidi was arriving. Baz looked at her pityingly.

"Shouldn't if I was you, love. 'Es got a bad dose of beri beri all over his todger. Very nasty. Curse of the academic life," Baz said mysteriously.

Heidi looked at Damien on the carpet, naked, sweating, his face screwed up in pain, and decided he wasn't so attractive after all. She turned and left. Dave sniggered. They'd only come to check if Damien had left, but had enjoyed a little interlude as well.

"Nice one, Bazza," he said and they sauntered away.

Damien rubbed his leg painfully, and got dressed. God, he was glad to be leaving this dump. There was something seriously wrong with the people here. They'd never appreciated him, but now he was going to a land of sunshine and applause.

He'd have Botox injections in a few years and be known as the Peter Pan of the West Coast. He'd have pecan pie with starlets, lime pie with adoring girls who knew his poems by heart (he'd decided to call the Penguin collection *The Dark Heart*); a Jacuzzi and steam room in his exquisitely furnished professorial apartment, perhaps an original Dali or two once the salary and royalties kicked in; he'd refurbish his wardrobe along incongruously chic lines – one day lumberjacks' skin tight jeans and jacket, the next a wafer thin beige Armani suit with wide tie and brogue shoes.

He would display a vast knowledge of classical music yet

attend new wave hip hop and punk concerts. His accent would be worshipped and people would invite him to cocktails just to hear the mellifluously undulating tones of his voice – sometimes earthy working class and sometimes the lounge lizard drawl of a disaffected upper class that both acknowledged and distanced itself from an ancient royal line. He'd be the Mick Jagger of poetry, only younger and prettier. People wouldn't be able to pin him down and he'd be the chameleon of the campus circuit – the mercurially talented poet everyone wanted a piece of.

His good mood restored, he closed the door for the last time and realised he didn't have anyone to say goodbye to. He knocked on Frank Finch's door but there was no reply and it was locked. For a moment he could have sworn he heard music inside, but he must have been mistaken.

Then he almost knocked on Mercedes Blonk's door. He thought it would be cool to just go in, throw her over the desk and have a last screw before he left Roebuck for good. She'd certainly be up for it after last time, but when he knocked he thought he could hear faint moans from inside that went quiet, and started up again, a young Asian voice saying, "I couldn't possibly do that. Surely it is illegal."

She'd probably left the World Service radio on. Oh well, it'll mean extra time to shop at the airport.

Chapter Thirty-Nine

Trev said not a word throughout the journey. Spinelli didn't seem to notice, or perhaps he preferred to do all the talking, so Trevor let him twitter on while he tried to think what to do. This little twerp was Cynth's lover and he said they were going to be married. For the second time Trevor considered the possibility of just asking them to stop the car, getting out and walking away. But it wasn't a real possibility. What used to be stubborn naivety now felt like resolve. OK, he might lose her, but not without a fight. He wondered who the hell this man was anyway. He was obviously wealthy and they'd called him General – perhaps he was with the Salvation Army.

When they arrived at the hospital, Boris and Boris stayed in the Lincoln while the General insisted on going to the shop to buy boxes of chocolates and bunches of flowers for Cynth. Trevor used this as an excuse to leave, and said the person he was visiting would be waiting. The General saluted and gave him his personal card.

"One days you iss coming to my country, I giff you one good jobs. Maybe Minister of Cultures or sometheengs. And you don't 'ave to kill nobodys. Hokay? My country she iss changing when I gets back. You theenk I 'ave these eyes of a wise prophet?" The General beamed his oily smile.

Trevor nodded then raced along the corridor to Cynth's ward. She was sitting up in bed, writing in a notebook. Trevor skidded to a halt at her bedside.

"Are you writing a poem?" Trevor asked.

She nodded.

"I hope it's as good as the others. They're really great. I've got your poems. The pink folder. I'll tell you about it later."

Cynth stared at him. This odd young man from her Creative

Writing group was full of surprises. During the night she had started to wonder if she had dreamed him, but now here he was again, with another surprise. He called her a great writer. He obviously liked her poems, but how did he get them?

She had successfully withdrawn from so much and had decided that numbness was preferable to anything else. This inevitably led to the thought that the ultimate numbness would be death. She had no belief in heaven, but did think that there was something strange about human consciousness that might not be extinguished. It might be that the only living tissue of her father was in her mind, but wasn't that a kind of afterlife? There was also the raw fact that she did not want to live. But now something had happened.

She wondered what the odd sensation she was starting to experience really was, and then it came to her. It was curiosity. It had been a long time since she felt properly curious. Curiosity meant engagement with the world from which she had been systematically withdrawing. Now it was beckoning her again. But to what? And with whom?

"Listen, there's not much time. Your fiancé's on his way," said Trevor.

Cynth looked at him amazed. Obviously he was mad. Had he really broken into her room and saved her life? Did he really have her poems? She had no idea to whom he was referring. Fiancé? She knew she'd been given a lot of Valium and perhaps that had affected her, or perhaps the overdose she had taken had damaged her brain. Also, this person seemed to think they were in some sort of a relationship. Had she missed something? A love affair that somehow took place in a parallel universe? She had hoped that the morning would bring greater clarity, but it was turning out to be weirder than anything she'd experienced before.

"He's getting you chocolates and flowers," said Trevor.

Chocolates? Cynth realised that she hadn't thought about chocolate for – how long now? – two days? Three? Her dreams had been vivid and Dad had been in them, but smiling. And, she now realised, there had been something reassuringly ordinary about the dreams. Meals, walking, nothing spectacular. No underlying current of urgent fear, no knot of panic, no ache permeating the painful detail of everyday life. Perhaps this strange lad really had helped her in some way. And she didn't even know his name.

"See, he gave me a lift here. To be honest, I don't know what you see in him. You're far too good for him. But I s'pose you love him. Do you?"

She didn't have a clue who he was talking about, but whoever he was, she certainly didn't love him, so she shook her head.

"So it was just a physical thing? Not just physical. I mean, I'm pretty liberal myself and spend most of my time thinking about the physical thing. Mostly with you, except when I'm desperate but …" Trevor was blushing fiercely. "Or is it money? He's obviously a rich bastard. Are you marrying him for money?"

Cynth shook her head again.

Trevor plucked up his newfound courage.

"Do you want me to get you away from him?"

Cynth nodded. He'd said he really liked her poems. She smiled.

It was all he needed. With a speed of thought and action that surprised them both, Trevor wheeled her bed to the side of the ward, taking care not to upset any of the tubes or drips attached to her. He pushed her through a side double door and left her beside a service lift.

"Back in a minute," he said.

He took the name tag from her wrist and went back to the ward and to the bed cubicle containing the snoring Professor Trevalyan. He opened the screen and pushed his bed into the place where Cynth's had been and put her chart, with her name on it, in the slot at the foot of Trevalyan's bed. Her things – a brush, a spare nightdress – lay on a chair by the bed. In his sleep Trevlayan moved and the rubber ring under his bottom squeaked a little. He smiled.

Trevor took off Trevalyan's wrist tag and replaced it with Cynth's, then left him and returned to her. He looked in a few cupboards and found a porter's coat, which he put on, then wheeled Cynth's bed into the lift and pressed the button. As the lift descended to the underground service area, he looked at her.

"I was wondering …" he said, then stopped, blushing.

She looked at him.

"Just a thought. I just wondered if you'd like to have full sexual intercourse with me. I mean not now, there probably isn't time or anything anyway, and you've got all those tubes and you've just tried to kill yourself, but maybe when you're feeling a bit better …"

"Yes," said Cynth.

Trevor appeared not to hear and blundered on.

"And if it was all right, I mean if we both liked it a lot, we could do it on a sort of regular basis with a view to … you know … I mean we could even get married one day or something, after we'd done it quite a bit. You could be Mrs Bottom. Oh, I'm Trevor Bottom. Pleased to meet you. You might want to think about it first, but do you like Yorkshire terriers? I suppose I should say I am, you know, in love with you and I've spent most of this first term imagining you naked and having sex with you. It's always very good. I mean in my imagination. In case you're worried about quality. Did you say yes?" He suddenly looked stunned.

Cynth nodded. She realised it was the first word she'd spoken for eight months.

Trevor's mouth opened. Then a smile spread across his face that made him look almost attractive. She'd said yes. Now he could do anything. A few minutes later, he was knocking on the door of the Lincoln. Boris opened the electric window.

"The General wants you to take her back to the campus. He told me to bring her," he said, and got in the car.

He directed them down to the underground service parking area, then got out and wheeled Cynth's bed into view. Boris and Boris were strong men, and between them they managed to lift Cynth and her drip onto the back seat.

"Where's the boss?" asked Boris.

"He's having a bit of an argument with the doctor about her leaving. He said to take Cynth back, then come and collect him."

Boris wavered and looked at Boris. The General would relish a fight with a doctor, and given they were in a hospital, the poor man wouldn't have far to go for treatment once the General had finished with him, but it was unusual for him not to want them to wait.

Trevor took out the card the General had given him and showed it to them.

"He must trust me, to let me travel with his fiancée, and after all he is a wise prophet, isn't he?" said Trevor with a smile and a wink.

Boris looked at Boris, who nodded. This kid had spunk. He was all right. In the old country they would have taken him on, shown him the ropes; extortion, pimping, a little drug work, protection, debt collecting, government work, such as the enhanced interrogation of dissidents (liberals called it torture). It would have been fun. He would have enjoyed it and become one of the boys. It was all too easy to slip into nostalgia in this Godforsaken country. Moments later the Lincoln was speeding away from the hospital.

Chapter Forty

Jeremy Pickles squirmed in his seat, clenching and unclenching his buttocks hundreds of times during his difficult conversation with the Chancellor.

Adam was furious and it was difficult to explain to him the near castration scene in his office without giving the impression that he was losing his grip. If nothing else, it was undignified to nearly lose your testicles in a fairly public manner. He badly needed to vent spleen on someone, and when Adam mentioned that Frank had been seen entering his office and should be removed as soon as possible, Jeremy sucked in his cheeks and knew he had his target. It was only a small thing, but having that piece of dead wood ejected from the campus would at least restore a little favour with the Chancellor.

"Leave it to me, Chancellor," he said and put down the telephone.

He immediately telephoned Frank. He had to wait a full minute before he was answered, and then no one spoke.

"Dr Finch, is that you?"

"Listen to the rising notes. Exquisite. I do think that all beauty is built upon fragility, the possibility of collapse," said Frank.

The sooner this old tosser was put out to graze on some funny farm, the better.

"Listen, Finch, after your disgraceful performance in the crematorium, for which you could be prosecuted for slander I might add, you are finished here. Your employment at Roebuck terminated there and then. You have brought this fine institution into disrepute. You have five minutes to gather your miserable belongings and get out." Jeremy slammed down the phone.

Fifteen minutes later he telephoned again.

"Why the hell are you still there?" he shouted.

"For one thing, the second movement of Brahms Sinfonia Number One in D Minor is just beginning. *Andante Sostenuto*. Another reason is it's my office. I've worked and taught and thought and talked and dreamed in here for thirty-one years," said Frank softly, conducting the music with his free hand.

Jeremy snapped down the telephone again and then called security.

"Get over to the English department and I want Frank Finch out of his office and off the campus in five minutes. I don't care if you've just been there!" And he slammed the phone down yet again.

Ten minutes later there was a knock on Frank's door. He ignored it. Another knock. Then voices.

"Dr Finch? Security. We know you're in there. Now you be a good boy and come out."

A pause. Another knock. Then keys rattling. Frank got up and bolted the door from the inside then pushed a chair against it under the handle. He sat at his desk and listened again to the music. The pipes were in fine form; they had become louder, more distinct, as if the whole structure of Roebuck was transforming into song, anticipating and perhaps celebrating or lamenting an impending event. The pipes were the arteries of the university, carrying its music from cell to cell, like a pulse, like a heartbeat. And if anyone had now told Frank that others couldn't hear it, he would have thought them deaf or deranged.

"I may be alone, but I have the music. The sounding of the spheres," he said aloud.

Behind him, a musical voice seemed to hear his thoughts, and said: "Sure, and those leprous noseholes who run this place cannot hear because they say you have no soul inside, only grey matter, because they don't know what it is to have a soul themselves."

And she was fully there now. Standing in front of the print of Van Gogh's *Sunflowers*. A little lined, but with bright quick eyes, a full figure and a knowingness that was attractive. She perceived his thought in a twinkle and smiled.

"If you weren't a married man I'd say touch me with soft, soft,

soft hands. Trust me, my longlashed eyes, my hand gentle. But what do you do now, Frank Finch?" she said in a lilting Dublin accent.

"I don't know, Molly. What should I do?"

"Well, Pickles is after you and that's a fact. But, my God, he's Mouth Almighty and has the hardest-boiled eyes of all the big stupoes I ever met. He's the king in this warren of weasel rats."

"Maybe I should just go quietly," said Frank.

"You stand your ground in these stoneheaps of dead builders and you'll be with your love. I know about love. And then these will all be inked characters fast fading on the frayed, breaking paper," said Molly Bloom, as he knew her to be.

"I'm not sure," said Frank.

"I'm sure. Pickles is a bag of corpse gas sopping in foul brine, fat of a spongy titbit, flash through the slits of his buttoned trouserfly. They're a quiver of minnows in this hole of bricks. Now look at him and no more turn aside to brood. There's a champion if ever I saw one," she said, turning and looking at … who?

There in the corner was the young man with dark curly hair holding a sword. He looked sternly at Frank and hit his own chest with a clenched fist. He spoke but the words were less clear than Molly's, words rusted by history:

"… *totamque infusa per artus mens agitat molem et magno se corpore miscet. Inde hominum pecudumque genus vitaeque volantum et quae marmoreo fert monstra sub aequore pontus.*"

Frank translated what he could hear: "One mind, infused, through every part, sustains. One universal, animating soul quickens, unites and mingles with the whole."

He felt it to be an expression of solidarity. It was Aeneas talking to him, giving him courage. Aeneas, who had been to Hades and fought with all manner of enemies and his own demons. He, Frank, wasn't alone, perhaps. They were here. Also another strange brooding young man in the corner, still muttering to himself as he did in the crematorium. It was Hamlet, of course, bent on his own dark course, but fascinating, engaging in monumental self-obsession, desperately trying to make some sense of life. And there, with the walrus moustache and fierce vulnerability, sitting on his filing cabinet, Friedrich Nietzsche, sternly contemplating the potted geranium Margaret had given Frank four years ago. He pointed to one of the many cards Frank had pinned on his wall. This one was a quotation from Nietzsche's *Daybreak*: *What is the best remedy? – Victory.*

Yes, thought Frank. Victory. That would be something. But how best to achieve it? Well, for one thing, he had to stand his ground. Molly had been quite clear on that. He turned and smiled at her. But something very strange had happened. She was still there, but she was no longer Molly Bloom. She was now a queen, quite short, in Egyptian headdress and golden gown, her eyebrows painted a fierce black, a slightly hooked nose. Cleopatra.

"That's my brave lord!" she said. "Victory indeed. You have immortal longings in you and will yet mock the luck of Caesar."

"Caesar. Is he here too?" asked Frank.

"He hides in his Tower. But he knows you are here. All the gods go with you. Upon your sword sit laurel victory, and smooth success be strew'd before your feet." Then she flickered, became Molly again and winked at him.

It was getting crowded in his office now, and he felt cheered. The pipes were playing an improvised and jolly military march, with a tenor saxophone flitting arpeggios around the beat. He felt strangely elated. All these characters here with him, helping him. He wished he could tell Margaret.

Someone was banging at the door but the noise seemed far off and he felt brave.

Chapter Forty-One

It was strange. General Spinelli put down the huge bunch of flowers and five boxes of Roses chocolates he was carrying, and looked around the ward. Cynth definitely wasn't there.

He went back to the nurses' station and was told that Cynth hadn't been moved. He went back. Brimley was snoring peacefully in the place where Cynth should have been. Then Spinelli saw the chart at the bottom of the bed. It had Cynth's name on it. And there were her things on the chair. He looked at Brimley's wrist tag and it had her name on it too. He felt the old familiar ball of anger in his belly start to swell and turn to bile, then rise in his throat. How could he be wise when these bastards constantly fucked with him? Who did they think they were dealing with? At this moment 'they' included practically everyone at Roebuck.

He prodded Brimley hard in the chest and he awoke halfway through a deep snore that turned to a choke and splutter. The tubes attached to his wrist trembled. He spluttered again and automatically reached for the oxygen mask, but Spinelli stopped him.

"Professor, I iss asking you one times. Where she iss?"

"I beg your pardon?" asked the bewildered Brimley.

Spinelli pulled one of the tubes out of his wrist roughly. A dribble of saline splashed across his chest.

"I want the nurse," said Brimley.

"Not yet. You 'ave one whole barrel of nurses when I am doing the finishings with you. My girl, my wife to be, this one girl who leesten to me, the bellissimo Cynth: What you 'ave done with her and why you are making the monkeys of me, wearing her names? You think I am the big stupid arseholes you can pisspot over and laughing ha ha ha!? You are thinking I am not good enoughs for 'er? No, I know now – you think you can 'aves her for yourselves, yes?"

Brimley was staring at his nametag in bewilderment.

"I have no idea what you are talking about, Mr Spinelli," he said.

Spinelli slapped him hard around the face.

"Now you insult me and my mother and my family's and my great name. I am one *Generali* Vittorio Carbella Vincentio Carlos Juanta Manuel Spinelli. You steal my wimmins because you are the jealous ones. I telling you, Doctorr Feench is the honly 'onest mens I is meeting in this one Roebuck University. All these others are smelling like the cheesyboards." The General's face was now flushed and working overtime to produce a kind of oily fury.

"Finch is a piece of the past we are about to jettison," said Brimley. "I can assure you that ..." But already he knew his haughty tone was a profound mistake.

I really do shovel very, very deep holes for myself, he thought, as the General took a towel from the bedside and stuffed it in his mouth, then took the drip tube and tied him across the arms and chest to the metal bed frame. Brimley thought that would be that but had little idea of how, once the General was wound up, it took a great deal to unwind him. He needed to take pain to its logical conclusion.

He pulled the oxygen tube from the mask and plugged it into the rubber ring beneath Brimley's troublesome posterior, then switched it on. He looked with satisfaction as the ring started to swell. Then he lit a cigarillo and grinned.

"Please stop this," said Brimley, thinking that life had been pointedly ruthless to him during the last thirty-six hours. Twice he had been tied up by people who then proceeded to cause him excruciating pain in parts of his body that should be intensely private. When would it all end?

Spinelli blew smoke in Brimley face and, once his eyes had cleared, the little General had gone, but the rubber ring was now of frightening proportions and was making his back arch into a semi circle that was so painful it squeezed all the breath from his lungs. It wasn't fair. His back was going to break and it would be very difficult to sack people when you had to rely on them to open doors for you. He wondered if the university would pay for an electric wheelchair. After all, this was a sort of work-related incident.

The sweat poured from him as he felt his spine about to snap, then the cushion – now the size of a Massey Ferguson tractor tyre – exploded with a window-rattling bang that had the alarming effect of propelling the whole bed forward at great speed and with the roaring rasp of a Gargantuan fart. It shot across the ward and slammed into the bed of Miss Alice Crushbank, eighty-seven years old and on her third hip replacement. She was asleep and dreaming of *Gone With the Wind*, thinking that Bette Davis would have made a better Scarlet O'Hara. More dangerous. More risqué.

The force of the collision stopped Brimley's bed but not Brimley himself; the drip tube holding him to the bed snapped and he was hurled onto the prostrate Miss Crushbank, who awoke to find him firmly on top of her, his wet face against hers, his body quivering on her, tubes trailing from it like alien arteries. She wished she'd put her teeth in.

This was the moment that Mrs Trevalyan had chosen to visit her husband. She had been told in lurid detail on the telephone by Baz about Jeremy's strange predicament in his office. Dr Duff had telephoned her and warned her never to have physical contact with her husband again, which she thought a shade ironic given that there had been so little physical contact for years anyway. And what little there had been was unmemorable. Now, as she watched Jeremy flapping around on top of an elderly woman with his little white legs waggling in the air like a sun-starved insect, she decided her marriage was well and truly over. It was a relief.

Two nurses came running and, to the great disappointment of Miss Crushbank, pulled Brimley off her. Mrs Trevalyan left.

"Some o' the boogers. Can't leave it alone for a minute," said a large nurse, an Irish girl called Patsy. "Looks a nasty piece of work. Funny little eyes. Sort of rodenty."

"He's obviously raving," said her friend. "Attacking poor old Alice. Could have killed her. Needs calming down. Better give him a you-know-what."

Before Brimley could gather his wits to reply, he was flipped over by Big Patsy as if he was a feather and had his comfort pants slipped down. The other nurse quickly prepared a syringe and Brimley had a powerful solution of bromide and Valium injected into his buttocks. The effect was immediate and he started dribbling as he tried to protest his innocence.

Chapter Forty-Two

Frank had taken twelve painkillers so far today and was about to take another. It had become an unconscious act. He held it to his mouth when he felt a hand on his.

"Not now. There's no need," she whispered.

He caught his breath and looked around. She wasn't there. But he felt a surge of strength that stilled the great wash of weariness starting to come over him. He rallied and felt the wolves were coming. He could almost smell them. *Very well. Let them come for me. I am not alone any more.* Sure enough, a few moments later, he heard voices outside his door.

The murmuring became more urgent as Jeremy Pickles remonstrated with what were meant to be two of his crack security team. He had seen them on CCTV appearing to prevaricate. Why the hell didn't they just use their master keys, then go in and dispatch Finch? Finally he decided that if you wanted to win a war you had, unfortunately, to occasionally put in an appearance yourself. He was told that Dr Finch had bolted the door from the inside.

"Then break it down. What are you waiting for?"

"Conflict of professional interests, Mister Pickles," said Baz, eating a bacon sandwich.

Dave nodded sagely and spat in the empty fire bucket.

"What are you talking about? What conflict of professional interests?"

"Well, on the one hand we are security guards. We are also trained first aiders in the ambulance service. Now if we was to break down said door and Dr Finch was on the other side, we could well cause him bodily harm, thus violating one code of practice whilst simultaneously fulfilling another. You see our problem? Security. Health and Safety. Unhappy bedfellows."

Dave nodded again and stared at Pickles, who was beginning to find him a little intimidating. Pickles thought of Boris and Boris holding him over his desk and his fear-withered testicles. Bottle the fear. Cap it, he said to himself.

"Then tell him to stand away from the door," Pickles said.

Baz looked at Dave and they both shook their heads. Clearly the Registrar had no notion of the subtleties of their position.

"No can do," said Baz, wiping his lips and belching slightly as he tapped his stomach. "I mean, it doesn't get to the nub of our Health and Safety dilemma, does it?"

"Don't even touch the nub," agreed Dave.

"Because, even if we assume that the good doctor does move to a position of relative safety, and we'd only have his word for that, the door being a visual impediment to confirmation, but even assuming he does, you have to appreciate that this isn't just a door, my friend."

"Of course it's just a door," said Pickles.

"No. It's also a fire prevention utility like this emergency bucket." He dropped his sandwich crust into it and belched again, baconly. "Imagine we knock it down, what's to stop a firestorm from blowing straight through and into this corridor, thus endangering the lives of hundreds?"

"But there is no fire!" said Pickles.

"No, because the fire prevention utility is doing its job. You see how it works?"

"Constantly on it. The job," said Dave, and spat in the fire bucket again.

Jeremy was getting worried. It wasn't right. He should be barking orders and these two morons should be jumping to attention, fearful for their jobs. Why were they behaving as if they were in charge and he was mentally deficient?

Chapter Forty-Three

Cynth was able to walk and appeared to be much revived by her recent adventure. After Boris and Boris dropped them off at Roebuck, Trev decided they should go to his room. The General would be looking for her and she'd be safer here.

She sat on his sofa bed and smiled.

"Are you hungry?" Trev asked. "I've got some Pot Noodles in the kitchen, if no one's pinched them. They're only a bit past their sell-by."

"I'm OK," said Cynth, and realised, with a pang of surprise, that food was not uppermost in her mind. She felt a sense of release and wondered if she should trust it.

There was a moment's awkward silence. Everything suddenly felt embarrassingly intimate. The room seemed ridiculously small.

"Funny this, eh?" he said. "I mean, I know you're used to being in bedrooms with loads of different blokes, but it … I'm sorry, I shouldn't have said that. Things just slip out. Always been like that. Sometimes I think I should just keep my mouth shut and only write."

"I like it when you talk," said Cynth.

Trev beamed. He sat next to her and they started chatting. It all came so ridiculously easy. He told her about an imaginary childhood friend called Alf whom he used to confide in, and one day Alf surprised him by saying that he thought Trev was *his* imaginary friend.

Cynth told him about her dad and found that the truth started to seep back as she spoke, at least *her* truth: that he was sometimes a bit strict and was not nearly as good looking as he had become in her imagination. Somehow that made her feel better. The grief was, if anything, keener, but it *belonged* to her now rather than her feeling overwhelmed by it.

Trev and Cynth discovered they had a great deal in common: a love of marmite soldiers; atheism; The Red Hot Chili Peppers; frequently losing touch with reality (whatever that was); a profound disappointment with university; a fear of crowds and earwigs. And, of course, a love of literature.

Trev told her how difficult he found everyday life, the million small lacerations to the spirit, the sheer problem of having a consciousness. And to his amazement, she didn't back away thinking he was mentally ill or a pretentious turd. In fact she said that simply hearing him say it made her feel better about herself. Trev also said that he thought about sex every 2.3 seconds, but Cynth was less communicative here. Trev suspected that this was because of her vastly superior experience and an admirable desire on her part not to make feel him feel inadequate. There would be time to ask about her bizarre choice of lovers. Now was not it.

Mostly the talk rolled between them like a wave, sometimes playful, amusing, sometimes hinting at depths. It was eldritch. Magic was in the air.

While they talked, a lot of wheels were turning. The Editor of the *Independent* had read with great interest Roy Fish's letter detailing Spinelli's arrival at Roebuck. He made a few inquiries, slept on it and now decided there was a story there. Possibly a big story that might run and unravel layers of iniquity. It had that feel about it.

He telephoned Dr Frank Finch, Spinelli's supervisor, and was told that he'd have to speak up because Brahms Sinfonia Number 1 in D Minor Op. 68 was just beginning and they were all going to have a cup of tea and listen.

"Who are you all?" asked the Editor, and was told Molly Bloom, Hamlet, Nietzsche, Aeneas, and now Richard the Second and Walt Whitman. Dr Finch said they were having trouble getting Whitman to shut up as he kept declaiming the Body Electric in a loud frontier boom, but Nietzsche was cleverly engaging him in a discussion about the meaning of art and things were quietening.

The Editor hung up and sent two of his best reporters and a photographer.

The news editors of Channel 4, Sky News and the BBC had received similar letters and already their gaudy TV vans were on the road for Roebuck. Even from beyond the grave, Roy Fish was keeping busy.

In his office, Frank was feeling dizzy with the music and chatter and having so many dear and illustrious friends there. Then he heard that something was wrong. There should be no percussive thumping in the Brahms piece, and in any case it was out of time, playing an odd sort of 5/8 beat. He realised it was someone hammering at the door.

"Finch, just stop this ridiculous nonsense and come out of there!" yelled Jeremy Pickles.

Frank ignored him.

"If you don't come out I shall call the police and have you thrown out!"

Frank wondered what to do. A figure appeared at his shoulder and whispered. Frank smiled.

"Thou bawdy toad-spotted gudgeon! Thou mewling folly-fallen popinjay!" he shouted at the door.

"What did you call me?" asked the bewildered Pickles.

Hamlet whispered in Frank's ear again.

"Thou spongy lily-livered mammet! Thou frothy sheep-biting wagtail!" Frank informed him.

Hamlet was rolling on the floor, his eyes gushing tears of laughter. He'd never been so happy. He appeared to have forgotten all about his poor dead father, his wayward mother, scheming stepfather, and poor, dead Ophelia.

"OK Finch. That's it. I'm calling the police. Do you hear?"

Molly Bloom appeared at Frank's side.

"Tell him to shove his ugly little dangler up his leprous nosehole, the little scrap of urinous offal," whispered Molly, her eyes dancing with mischief.

Frank smiled.

"Pickles, shove your ugly little dangler up your leprous nosehole, you little scrap of urinous offal," said Frank, amazed at himself.

He could hear laughter from behind the door. Clearly, whoever was with Pickles found it amusing. Pickles himself was far from entertained. He was rapidly stoking up an impotent rage, so when his mobile phone trilled the first few bars of *William Tell* he snapped: "Yes, what the bloody hell do you want?!"

He paled as he heard the Chancellor's voice.

"What I want, Pickles, is for you to stop this now and get control of the situation," said Adam Bittermouth, hiding his own increasing sense of alarm.

Adam's world appeared to be slipping out of control. Could it be that the Dark Invader himself was up to something? Some scheme, plotting some nefarious gravitational disaster. As if in answer, Adam saw on one of the CCTV screens people piling out of vans and into the Bittermouth Arts Block. People who shouldn't be there. People with cameras and equipment. Strangers.

For a terrible moment he thought he might have to leave the Tower to take charge, but the notion made him feel nauseous and he grabbed the anchor handles on his desk for ballast. He looked at the ceiling. It was still there and about the right distance away. The workmen had also finished and his reflecting screen was above the roof. He was safe.

Pickles would have to go once this crisis was past. The ship needed tightening. The Tower needed strengthening. Or even …yes … another tower! Bigger, stronger, taller. The university was making oceans of money. He could easily afford it. And a golden bridge connecting the two, so he could move between them. And an electronic fence surrounding the grounds. Only those with special passes could enter. Or people would have implants in their bodies that would electronically trigger the gates. That would keep the strangers out.

Students (the diminishing few) would have to pay an extra two thousand a year for the implant. The government had opened the top up fees floodgates so he could charge what he liked, and people were so stupid that they really thought if they paid more they got more. Einstein had known that. What was it? There were only two infinities – the universe and human stupidity, and he wasn't sure about the universe.

Chapter Forty-Four

The corridor outside Frank's room was now like a hive of bees on amphetamine. Reporters, photographers and TV crews were vying for space. In a sense they were the event and there was a great deal of filming and interviewing of each other, given that not too much seemed to be actually happening.

Jeremy Pickles was a very worried man. His plump hamster cheeks were waxy with sweat as he tried not to have his picture taken. This wasn't the national glory he had imagined for himself. One of the journalists, a pretty redhead called Chance, tried to get something from Baz and Dave.

"So have you actually met the tyrant?" she asked.

"Oh yes," said Baz.

He eyed her approvingly. He didn't have a clue who she was talking about, but he sensed that, for the moment, he had her attention. She had full lips and dangerous eyes. He'd like to see her tuck into a hot cannelloni.

"Don't say anything," snapped Jeremy, but Dave led him away in a gentle armlock.

"And what's he like?" she asked.

"Oh, what you might expect from a tyrant. Extremely tyrannical. Wholesale slaughter, infanticide, demonic rituals, buggery on a scale that would make your eyes water. You name it."

Chance thought this man was more interested in her breasts than a serious investigative news report on an international despot, but he would be worth keeping in reserve. She passed him onto her number two, an equally attractive blonde called Kirsty, to whom Baz launched a lurid and detailed version of how he and Dave had found the Professor of Quality Assurance in this very department in a state of debauched and unholy depravity, tied to a desk with a rubber tube up his Chadwick End.

Jeremy listened with growing horror. Dave smiled at him.

The bustle increased as another camera crew arrived. Chance knocked on Frank's door.

"Dr Finch, may I have a word with you?" she asked.

On the other side of the door Frank listened.

"I'm a television reporter and would like to ask you a few questions."

Frank felt nervous. Should he talk to these noisy people in the corridor? He felt a tickle in his left ear. It was Friedrich Nietzsche's huge walrus moustache as he leant close to whisper.

"*Mit der Schneide dieser Worte, gibst Du Hoffnung für unsere Herzen.*"

Frank translated to himself: With the sword of these words, you give hope to our hearts.

Nietzsche nodded, his brow furrowed and his lips grim, and then he walked back to Whitman to explain to him that God was not out in the prairies, nor in the human heart, but well and truly dead. Frank felt encouraged.

"What do you want to know?" asked Frank.

"General Spinelli – why has the university allowed him to study here?"

A very strange thing happened.

The mere mention of the odious gargoyle's name ignited in Frank's heart a flame of anger. He suddenly felt a well of bravado and indignation that could not be suppressed. There were things that had to be said. If it was to be his swan song, then so be it. He would sing it well. He cleared his throat and, behind him, they all stopped to listen – Hamlet, Molly, Aeneas, Whitman, Nietzsche, and a host of shimmering others.

"The university allowed Spinelli to come to here for one simple reason: he paid them a great deal of money. If you search the accounts properly, I'm sure you'll find this to be the case. I would start with the Registrar – money usually goes through him. Name of Pickles. Looks like a hamster."

In the corridor Jeremy reddened until he thought his cheeks

would burst into flames. Chance double checked levels with her sound man. This was starting to sound juicy.

"You think that Roebuck might really have been involved in some sort of … inappropriate dealing?" she asked.

"Ha!" exploded Frank with a venom that made him jump. "Inappropriate! Thereby hangs a tale. Roebuck is a disgrace throughout. The traditional idea of a university as a place of learning, where ideas may be exchanged, where young people come to flex their intellectual muscles and have the time and space to read and think, has been replaced by a seedy and vulgar philistinism. From its peeling paint to that ridiculous phallic Tower of Light.

"The government burdens the young with debts that turn them into mere consumers, and Roebuck takes the money and offers them a trivialized ragbag of non-sequiturs.

"The Classics have been replaced by a study of trash magazines; Art has been exchanged for advertising. We have degrees in housekeeping and car maintenance; degrees in tattooing and cosmetics; MAs in traffic control and home baking; PhDs in pest control and knitting. Literature has been usurped by doodling and theorized grocery lists; Science has been usurped by big game hunting for corporate grants.

"There is no joined-up thinking at Roebuck, or indeed at many other universities."

Frank took a deep breath. There was no stopping him now.

"Universities like this are run by middle management bureaucrats who don't know their Three Rs from their elbows and for whom thought is a foreign country. I know not whether they are naturally stupid or if they've taken one of their own courses."

In the corridor Jeremy had taken more than enough.

"Shut the fuck up!" he bellowed at the door. "Shut the fuck up, you mad old prick!"

It looked and sounded great on film; as the cameras whirred and hummed, Pickles looked like a man about to snap. It would make arresting television.

"If that lavatorial rumbling comes from our illustrious

Registrar, then I think he somewhat proves my case."

Many of those gathered outside applauded Dr Frank Finch. Jeremy didn't. He started hammering on the door.

Dave and Baz were on him.

"Do you mind, Baz?" Dave asked his colleague.

"Be my guest."

Dave head-butted Pickles, who fell like a brick, his nose flattened and already twice its normal width even before he hit the floor.

"You're a diamond, Bazza," said Dave.

"Where is Spinelli now, Dr Finch?" asked Chance.

"In hell, I hope. But you might also search the many new buildings in Roebuck that have doubtless sprung up in the past few days. The Idi Amin Snack Bar, possibly, or the Pol Pot Leisure Centre? Perhaps he's sipping cognac in the Holocaust Eatery or finding children to murder in Goebel's Crèche. Or there's the Tony Blair Research Centre for Self Advancement and the George Bush Peace Through War Building. Take your pick."

This guy is worth his weight in prime time, thought Chance as every fresh insult was recorded. Somehow, the camera's unblinking focus on the locked door gave Frank's words a solemnity. It was like a weird Becket play.

Then suddenly it went quiet.

Chapter Forty-Five

Trev started to feel uneasy.

"I have to go and see if someone is OK. If anyone knocks on the door, don't answer," he said to Cynth with what he hoped was a caring but manly authority.

She leaned forward and kissed him. It was a warm kiss, made sweeter through anticipation, and because hours of talking had created a small but exquisite world they both liked inhabiting.

As he approached the English department corridor in the Bittermouth Arts Block he knew something was wrong. All the bustle and wires and people coming and going ... it was ominous. The throng was at its most dense outside Frank's door. Trev approached and hoped that Dr Finch was all right.

Frank suddenly felt tired. He went to his desk and sat down, as he had thousands and thousands of times during the past thirty-one years. He looked out of the window, the great hideous towering infernal obscuring what had once been a view of tennis courts and sports fields. He used to enjoy watching students walking, kissing, playing sports, the seasons arriving and departing. Sometimes he would bring in Jemma and take her for a lunchtime walk around the fields. Professor Trevalyan then arrived and banned all pets from the department, only grudgingly allowing guide dogs.

"Why are these people so awful? They don't even seem to be happy," Frank said aloud.

"Don't trouble about it," she said, and her hand was on his shoulder.

"I'm very tired," he said.

"I know, my darling."

"Did you hear me? I did a great deal of shouting," he said, smiling.

"Yes. I heard. But that's enough silliness for now. We've got a lot to do, a lot to catch up with. I have things to show you."

He got up slowly and she took his arm. She always walked on his left. They got to the door. He turned and looked around.

"They've gone now," she said.

"But what about all those outside?"

"We won't bother about them."

And they walked out and through the hushed noise and bustle and clatter and silent shouting and fuss. Frank recognised the boy who was in love and smiled at him. The people let them through.

"How far is it?"

"Not far," Margaret said.

Trev felt a warmth, like a thermal heat draft, as he approached Frank's door. For a moment he could have sworn he saw Dr Finch, but he must have been wrong.

"Hello pervy," said Dave.

Trev ignored him and turned to Baz.

"Open the door," he said.

Baz looked at him incredulously.

"Just open the soddin' door with your master key," said Trev.

Something in his voice, something about him that was new, made Baz take his master key from his pocket and turn it in the lock. Trev shoved against the door.

"Help me," he said to Dave.

Dave frowned but Baz nodded at him. Dave barged the door, and the bolt cracked away inside. Flashbulbs popped as Trev entered. He went over to Frank on his chair, slumped forward on his desk. He knew he was dead. He touched his hand and was surprised that it was still warm. He had no idea what a dead person's hand should feel like. He leaned close and whispered.

"Thanks for the book, Dr Finch. Thanks for everything."

"His heart," someone said, and suddenly the room was full. This was a real story now. There was a body. It was all a question of who could claim they were first to see it. And then the fun would really begin – who could be blamed? What angle was best:

Tragic Victim? Reluctant Hero? Arguably it could be construed as murder – sweet old duffer hounded to an early grave. Or perhaps a more dignified approach with Frank as guardian of high culture against the corporate Philistines now running our universities. This was starting to have all the marks of a good old scandal.

Trev walked away. Maybe it was Dr Finch's heart, but who broke it? He thought he knew. It was this bloody place. What should be a palace of dreams had become a pit of rather drab insects. Some of them could bite, but they were a shabby, pathetic little bunch really.

He and Cynth had been humiliated, used and abused, and were getting into thousands of pounds of debt to be taught by a bunch of tossers more interested in their own inane little reputations. And now Dr Finch was gone too.

As he stood in the lift for the ground floor, he could hear the gurgling of the pipes. He knew what they were saying now. It seemed so obvious. They were asking to be put out of their misery. And they were asking him to do it.

He felt clearheaded. He went to see if Cynth was OK. She was asleep. Good. It would all be over when she woke. He pushed the stray lock of hair from her forehead and left a note saying: *Won't be long. Glad you're here. Two or three Yorkshire terriers? I love you. Trev XXXX.*

He took his backpack from the top of the small wardrobe and went to the kitchen that no one ever used. The bottles and tin cans were still there under the sink where he had left them. He still didn't quite believe they'd work, but he'd soon find out. Those two weird blokes in the library had been pretty sure, and they seemed to know what they were talking about. He put some fuses made from shoe laces in his pocket and set out. He felt strangely calm.

And on the six o'clock news that Trev was missing, Frank Finch was becoming a national figure.

Chapter Forty-Six

Cynth awoke and felt much better. She read Trev's note and, although she didn't understand the reference to Yorkshire terriers, the words "I love you" resonated in her.

I love you. It was so absurdly simple, but it felt like a rock in a storm. And he liked her poems. He really liked them. She was the fat girl, Daddy's girl. But Daddy had gone and all she had felt was his absence and her weight. Now there was something different. Now she was back, back, back. She had become strong. Because someone died, the world didn't stop. Not unless you allowed it to. Grieve deeply but not for too long. She had no idea where that thought came from but it helped. It had the simplicity of truth. She got up and felt the need for air.

The General was in a spitting rage. Cynth was not in her room and he couldn't find Pickles anywhere. He felt murderous towards Boris and Boris for being fooled by Trev. He paced up and down the silken carpet in his apartment. Boris and Boris stood by the door looking at their shoes.

"Where she is being, my Cynth, eh? Where? They think they can play the monkeys with me. I tellings you someone in this place is getting their ears chopped up into the mincefingers. Iss big hinsult to me! I iss overwormed with hanger."

He dropped his cigarillo on the carpet and crushed it with his heel, then turned to Boris and Boris. They were the only ones on whom he could vent his fury. The Wise Prophet had finally completely choked to death in a red mist.

"And you twos, this one Heenlgish Bottom boy making the lemon harseholes of you. How you are believings him? You are two times more stupid than you iss looking."

He approached Boris and looked up at him. Although he could

barely reach his face, he pointed a finger, which just about reached the tip of his nose.

"Maybe I needing some new mens, 'uh? Maybe you don't 'ave thees one big ballses for thees jobs no more. You certainly don't 'aving no fucking brains."

An arm came from behind and held his hand tight. No one threatened Boris when Boris was around. Not if Boris had anything to do with it. Not even the General.

"Wha the fuck! Lemme go! You breaking my feengers."

Boris crushed his hand until he could feel the bones about to splinter, then let go. Spinelli fell to his knees holding his damaged digits. Now his rage was matched only by his fear. He would have these two crimped and carved, halved and quartered, but he'd have to wait. He looked up at their impassive bulks. Their eyes showed nothing.

"Hokay. We forgetting thees meestake. Hokay now. We go to see eef Peeckles is back. I making thees bastard pay. You two good boys can 'ave some fun with 'im, eh? Bring one battery and the cow prodding."

Ten minutes later the General was in Pickles' office, blowing on his painfully swollen fingers. Boris and Boris stood by the door impassively. But where was Pickles?

How could they know that Jeremy Pickles was in a builder's skip, concussed and with a horribly mangled nose?

In the arts block journalists had kept tripping over his unconscious body. He'd fulfilled his part in the drama and was of no further use, so the ever helpful Baz and Dave carried him outside and dumped him with the other rubbish.

In the Tower of Light, Adam was so intent on following the horrendous events in the English department that he didn't see Trevor Bottom enter below.

No one stopped him. The security guards, usually so vigilant in protecting Adam from the world, had gone to the Bittermouth Arts Block to see what the fuss was all about.

Trev found the boiler room down a few steps and, whistling

while he worked, checked the wires on all the power consoles. He went outside, took off his shoe and smashed the fire alarm glass. Then he pulled the lever and the siren screamed.

Up on the top floor Adam listened to the alarm in a state of palpitating terror. Alarms, unpredictable behaviour, perverse passions. The cameras told him that the world was ending – everyone was where they shouldn't be, uncontrollable events were happening, chaos was coming like an army of phantoms. Of course, he knew what it really was. Such a grand catastrophe could only be the work of someone, or something, demonic; something that was after Adam. The Dark Invader was making his move. He would use weapons, fire and smoke, explosions, and gravity. His hideous angels would carry banners with *ADAM'S MORTALITY* etched on them. It wasn't fair. Hadn't he built this Eden, this world of rewards for loyalty to him? Hadn't he reached out into the blankness and tried to feel the hand of God?

He was so agitated that he didn't see Trev, floors below him, place tin cans (one Safeway peaches and one Asda bean tin – Trev couldn't afford the overpriced things in the university's Roebuck Supermarket with its Bittermouth's own brand goods) on the power consoles.

Trev realised he didn't have anything to light them with so he went up to the library coffee bar and asked Helen, who was smoking a cigarette, if he could have some matches. She gave him a book of Roebuck Allumettes and, in return, he told her that it might be best if she were to stay well away from the Tower of Light. Then Trev returned.

He decided upon a trial run. He put one of the smaller explosive devices in a metal filing cabinet, lit the fuse, and retreated to what he thought was a safe distance. He crouched and waited. Nothing. He approached the filing cabinet gingerly and carefully opened the cabinet drawer. The fuse had died halfway through. It had been too long. He cut a shorter fuse and lit it. Immediately there was an impressive explosion that blew him off his feet and hurled him onto the power console, crushing a miniature statue of the Tower of Light.

"Shit!" he said through blackened lips.

For a moment he thought he'd gone blind, and then he realized he still had his eyes closed. His ears rang with a sort of mad Nirvana punk-type aria. Maybe the fuse shouldn't be quite that short. He went into the toilet to check the damage. The front of his hair was stubble. His lips were black and his eyebrows and eyelashes were gone, so that he looked startled.

He changed the length of the fuses, lit them and walked away. It would take a while. He had time. He could watch from a safe distance.

Chapter Forty-Seven

The General looked through Pickles' window at the library and the Arts Block, which housed his dreams but now seemed like a mocking granite epitaph.

He could feel the old drives returning: rage, a bottomless vindictiveness at the world for not adoring him without his having to force things. In the old days he would drive into a town with his Band of Brothers and have a purge – fires, smoke, a few random killings. Fun with young girls. Afterwards he always felt better, relaxed, almost calm. He took a last drag on his cigarillo and flicked the butt into a large Oriental pot full of coloured sands beneath the window.

Then he saw her. Cynth was walking on the little path behind the Arts Block towards the stream. The General smiled. At last something was going right for him. He turned to Boris and Boris then looked down at Cynth.

"Bring her to me," he said.

Ten minutes later Cynth stood between Boris and Boris facing the General. He smiled at her with a hint of malice.

"My luff, why you are not comings to me when I say? You are 'aving the sometheengs better to did?"

She stared at him.

"I am asking you thees questions. I like it when you leesten to me, but when I asking thees fucking questions you answering. Hokay?"

She continued to stare.

"You weel talk, if I 'ave to …" He stepped forward and was about to hit her when she leaned back and head-butted him full in the face. His eyes crossed and he went down like a stungunned sheep.

Boris and Boris remained impassive, though they were both

thinking there was more to Cynth than met the eye, if that was possible. The newly crossed eyes, in the General's case.

Spinelli struggled to his feet and looked in amazement at Cynth. No woman had ever dared hit him back, let alone head-butt him. His dazed and fractured thoughts slowly reassembled as he took it in. He took a black-handled knife from his pocket and flicked the blade out. It had a vicious curve. He thrust it forward at Cynth's belly. But before it reached her, a large hand snaked forward and held the General's wrist so tightly he thought it would snap. Boris met his eyes. The knife clattered to the floor. Cynth picked it up and looked at the blade. She held it close to the General's face and his eyes swam with fear. Boris now held his other hand too. This bitch was going to slit his throat.

With a deft flick of the blade Cynth neatly sliced off one half of the General's moustache, which plopped to the floor like a large sweaty fly.

"Pathetic little cretin," Cynth said, then threw the knife across the floor and calmly walked from the room, closing the door quietly behind her.

The General's mind reeled from what had just happened. The world was changing moment by moment and he was losing all control of it. This insult was unthinkable, unbearable. There would have to be blood and pain to restore order of some kind. Then he would get out of this absurd place as soon as possible.

Boris and Boris let go of his wrists. He stepped back and took out a small revolver, aiming it at Boris, then at Boris.

"One at a time. Now I teachings you what 'appen you when playings the clever bastard with your General. You want in the 'ead or the gutses?" His little eyes thickened with oily purpose.

Boris and Boris remained impassive. They looked briefly at the General then out of the window.

"Hokay. I givings you both. 'Eads and gutses," said Spinelli.

He was angry that these buffoons showed no reaction now that their deaths were seconds away. This was usually the moment he loved, just before someone died or was going to be in unspeakable pain, and they could do nothing about it. Their eyes showed everything, as if their whole personality squeezed up into a little circuit of fear that shone from a wide rabbity stare. Boris and Boris, however, seemed indifferent. They were either extremely tough, or stupid, or philosophical. Whichever it was, they would soon be no more.

Spinelli squeezed the trigger.

There was a click.

He squeezed again.

Another click.

Boris reached into his pocket and took out six bullets. He threw them up and caught them on the back of his meaty hand, like playing jacks. He smiled at Spinelli, then at Boris.

"'Ey, I am just making the jestings with you, yes? Comprendez? I know you take thees bullets. I see you. Ha ha! We 'ave these good laughings. Just a lurk."

Boris wasn't impressed. He walked slowly over to the General and picked him up by the neck with one hand and lifted him, considerably, until their faces were level. The General squawked.

"'Ey! You stop now. We make one deal. Yes? Por favor. I giving you one million US dollars. And fresh wimmins when we get 'ome. Amigo. 'Ermano. Foockeen lemme go!"

Boris was interested in neither. He looked at Boris, who nodded, then he flipped the General over as if he were a doll and held him above the large pot beneath the window while Boris crouched and scooped some sand aside, then planted the General, head first, in the plantpot, patting the sand around his ears. Boris held him by his feet.

It took three minutes of twitching before the General was finally still. Boris let his legs go and they crashed down, the General's head still firmly embedded. His body made a boomerang shape. Boris wiped the sand from his hands and they both left the office.

In the Tower of Light a screech made Adam jump. He held on to his desk supports. *Make me feel real*, he whispered to himself, his throat parching. The screech was from the speakers on the wall.

"Hello? Hello? Is anyone there?"

Surely this was the Dark Invader himself, come to mock before the apocalypse. The voice might sound young and nerdy, but that didn't fool Adam. No, not him. He'd lived with the possibility of this moment for too long to be fooled. And if he answered? Surely he'd be lost. Talk with the Devil and you're in with the Devil. Maybe he'd go away. If he thought Adam wasn't there he might not bother.

"Hello? Can you answer if there's anyone there? Only I'm about to blow up this whole building and I'd hate to hurt anybody. If you get out now you'll be alright," the voice said.

A trick. It was a trick. Everything was a trick. You suffered and planned and plotted and dreamed and all the time *He* was there watching, spying, mocking. The Dark invader. "There. Just when you think you're getting somewhere I'll come along and – puff! It's all gone." It was unfair. Everything was

Slipping away
　　Slipping
　　　　I'm slipping away
　　　　　Slipping ...

But he wouldn't give in. Be strong, he thought. Don't let him know you're here. And even if he does, don't let him know you're scared. Fuck him.

So Adam said nothing, and a thousand steps below him Trevor went into the boiler house and lit the fuses, then left the building.

He stood about a hundred metres away and watched.

Just before the explosion, Trevor looked and saw Boris and Boris walking away from the Tower of Light towards the Bittermouth Gardens and out of the university. He shouted and waved. They both stopped and saw him and waved back. They even smiled. That was the last he saw of them.

It was spectacular. An almighty explosion that rocked the bowels of the building. Windows shattered and showered glass onto the Roebuck walkways beneath. Within a minute a fire had started and spread through the whole of the first floor. Flames licked and tossed and spread, consuming all the digital hardware that had recently been installed to help Adam Bittermouth realise his dream.

Trev stood with others and watched the flames. He could feel the heat on his cheeks even from here.

"Bloody hell!" he said. "I didn't think it would be that good."

A girl standing next to him gave him a strange look, then moved away. Cheap wiring and pipes that carried the central heating oil were no match for fire, but were excellent conductors of it, and soon the whole library was an inferno. Even the cowboy builder that Jeremy Pickles had contracted to do things on the cheap would have been surprised at how quickly and easily the building blazed.

This was a day made in heaven for the press and television people. Scandal, corruption, death … and now an apocalypse. Reporters exhausted their headlining abilities as they struggled to explain how it appeared to be raining gold for at least five minutes as millions of glass shards sparkled and glinted. Then the magnificence of the Tower itself imploding, floor after floor, collapsing like a universe sucking itself into oblivion. A large cloud of black smoke drifted high and settled like a gigantic and vaporous raven above, and inside in the darkness Adam thought, "Yes, He is come. He always comes."

Adam's body was never recovered, so perhaps he was right and the Dark Invader really had come and taken him, or allowed gravity to push him so far below he never stopped falling.

That's that, then, thought Trevor Bottom.

Chapter Forty-Eight

Cynth was feeling much better after her little stroll and head-butting the General. She was rehydrated, rested, excited about what might happen next. New feelings fluttered inside her and she let them come and go. More than anything, she felt free.

The door opened and Trev entered. He came straight to her and they held each other. She said nothing about his alarming appearance. They kissed. He could see she'd decided something.

"I think we should go to bed now," she said.

Alarm bells went off in Trev's head and his recent courage, some might call it madness, deserted him. He reddened.

"Maybe we should wait."

"No."

"I'd better have a shower and change my socks," he said.

But she was in charge for now.

An hour later they sat up in bed drinking diet coke. To Trev it tasted like champagne. A wide smile threatened to split his face. They'd actually done it and everything was all right. Better than all right. It was bloody brilliant.

"We have to go," he said.

"Where?"

"Maybe by the sea somewhere. Only we can't stay at the university. I seem to have destroyed quite a lot of it, and I think I might have killed a few people, but only accidentally."

"Let's go then," she said.

They dressed and went downstairs. The chaos of the campus was growing by the moment. Fire engines, police, the army. Shouting, screaming, wailing. The smell of dust and ashes and smoke. Both Trev and Cynth felt removed from it, as if nothing could touch them. Trev was astonished that he'd made so much happen so quickly.

"Might not be a bus today," she said.

Trev looked around. There was the General's Lincoln in the car park. They walked over. The keys were inside. The General hadn't believed anyone would have the audacity to steal his car. Trev got in.

"Suppose we get stopped?" Cynth said.

Trev took the General's card from his pocket and showed it to her.

"Iss this one roads to paradise, hamigo?" They both laughed.

"I have to do something first," she said.

She rushed back to her room and returned with a zipped bag which she held tightly on her lap. Minutes later she and Trev were driving out of the campus. No one tried to stop them. There was too much confusion. Trev honked as they left the university grounds and they laughed again. Cynth waved like the Queen at a few bemused security guards and students, and beamed a smile at Helen from the Midlands, who looked momentarily surprised, then waved back.

Jeremy Pickles had climbed from the skip and was sitting in a dazed, dust covered heap by the side of the road, looking at the smouldering ruins of the Tower of Light. It seemed like the ash pile of his ambition. He would never get to meet the great Adam. He would never implement the Final Solution. He would never bamboozle academics and frighten office staff ever again. He had seen the greatness of his moment flicker, or was it the moment of his greatness? It didn't matter. It was over.

Or was it? Perhaps now, with Adam Bittermouth surely gone forever there would be an opportunity to rebuild. They'd need someone to sort this mess out, and who better than he, the great fixer?

Perhaps ... then his thoughts were dashed, or rather drenched, by a huge gush of foul water as Trev and Cynth sped by through a small pond, created by a burst pipe from the explosion. Jeremy cursed the plumbers he'd brought in on the cheap. He looked around. There seemed to be a lot of burst pipes. He could see that fire officials were already looking at the debris, puzzling over the cheap fittings. Only a matter of time before the smoky trail led to him.

The resurrection of his dreams now seemed somehow damp and futile. What is the point? What *is* the bloody point?

As Trev and Cynth left the city, Damien was three thousand miles away in the arrivals lounge at Los Angeles airport. He minced towards one of the great curved windows and looked outside at the lights. God, this was going to be *soooo* good.

When he turned around Professor Chad Bishop was standing there. He wouldn't shake hands.

It took him just two minutes to say they'd received confirmation that Damien had plagiarised someone else's work. Copies of the originals had been scanned and faxed to them by one Trevor something-or-other from Roebuck University. He told Damien that he could pay his own fare home or go fuck himself in hell. Then he turned and left.

As Trev and Cynth got onto the motorway, a meeting was about to end which would determine Brimley Trevalyan's immediate future.

James Thurbuck was resident psychiatrist at the hospital and had just come to a decision. As he was telling his chief administrator: "The man has a history. He was found in a state of complete physical and mental collapse after some sort of sex ritual. Clearly capable of extreme self abuse. Positive danger to himself. And now, after the episode with poor Miss Crushbank, he's clearly a worrying danger to others. His wife wants nothing to do with him. Deranged, psychotic, sexually predatory and prone to violence.

"I have no choice. We'll have him committed and start drug therapy immediately. Largactil to begin. Valium too. I think he'll end up being a long-termer. Probably Broadmoor, the hospital for the criminally insane. The man shouldn't be allowed near decent people."

Trev and Cynth arrived at Kessingland on the Norfolk coast. There was a breeze. The North Sea looked grey but fresh. The beach stretched for miles either way. They got out of the car and took great lungfuls of air. They walked down to the shore.

Trev took the champagne cork from his pocket and threw it out to sea. Cynth took the sacred and terrible tin with Ely Cathedral on it from her bag. It no longer looked sacred. It no longer held terror. She hurled it as far she could into the waves. It splashed, bobbled for a moment, then sank from sight.

She turned and smiled at Trev. He smiled back and felt the smell of Roebuck leave his clothes and disappear on the breeze.

The End

Also Available from BeWrite Books

The House in the Riddle by Liza Granville

Sorrel and Mark, her controlling, apocalypse-obsessed husband, arrived at the ruined barn and cottage chosen by him to be their final refuge in the coming End of Days only to discover that the property has its own secrets. Can Sorrel use these to break free of her past and find a life for herself? In this novel the lives of the mismatched pair intersect with those of several equally odd characters as their drama is played out.

A well-written psychological thriller gripping to the last page.

ISBN 978-1-906609-14-6

Flawed by Tom Larsen

'Brass Balls' Riley is leading a settled life when a friend from his youth re-appears with a scheme to make one, last, big score. Riley carries off the caper with the not-altogether helpful assistance of his criminally impaired wife and their friend. Can the wily and resourceful Riley keep one step ahead of the police, the FBI, and the special investigators hired by the victim?

This is an intriguing tale, told primarily from Riley's point of view, reminiscent of Raymond Chandler in style. Beautifully crafted, it takes the reader into Riley's mind and his surroundings sympathetically and humorously. A first rate read.

ISBN 978-1-906609-18-4

Notes from the Lightning God by John W. Schouten

In the majestic Andes a civilization is torn apart by revolution, terror, murder and extortion. A rebel army vows to bring down a corrupt government, which is equally brutal in defending its own interests. Meanwhile defenseless peasants are swept up in the bloodbath.

Into the strangely peaceful town of Santa Rosita wanders Samson Young, a med-school dropout and budding anthropologist. Sam's well-intended efforts to get his bearings and win the trust of the villagers seem fruitless, doomed by superstition that casts him as a pale bringer of death and disaster. That is, until an accident of nature transforms him in their eyes into a savior. Their legendary Lightning God.

As the unbridled violence closes in around him and the people with whom he has cast his lot, Sam can only record the horror in futile field notes ... and count its victims.

In Notes from the Lightning God, good and evil reside impurely in shades of gray. Terrorists, soldiers, police and drug lords, more than purely evil, are hard-edged expressions of their times and struggles. Sam's allies and antagonists include a village priest in a crisis of faith, a precocious eight-year-old boy, an extortionist cop, a lady doctor with a mobile medical clinic, a pragmatic captain of industry and coca, a conflicted television star, and a spirited and seductive graduate student, who is destined to be the love of Sam's life ... or the death of him.

ISBN 978-1-906609-12-2

www.bewrite.net

Lightning Source UK Ltd.
Milton Keynes UK
29 December 2009

147971UK00001B/32/P